FROM THE NANCY DREW FILES

THE CASE: *Nancy is hunting the thief who snatched a top-secret chemical compound from a campus lab.*

CONTACT: Dean Jarvis *of Emerson College has asked the teen detective to investigate.*

SUSPECTS: Karen Lewis—*her environmental group may be into more than peaceful protest.*

Sara Hughes—*the lab assistant had the best chance to steal the compound.*

Professor Maszak—*he alone knows the secret of the experiment.*

COMPLICATIONS: *Nancy tries to keep Ned out of the case, but whoever is after her has plans for Ned, too.*

Books in The Nancy Drew Files® Series

#1 SECRETS CAN KILL
#2 DEADLY INTENT
#3 MURDER ON ICE
#4 SMILE AND SAY MURDER
#5 HIT AND RUN HOLIDAY
#6 WHITE WATER TERROR
#7 DEADLY DOUBLES
#8 TWO POINTS TO MURDER
#9 FALSE MOVES
#10 BURIED SECRETS
#11 HEART OF DANGER
#12 FATAL RANSOM
#13 WINGS OF FEAR
#14 THIS SIDE OF EVIL
#15 TRIAL BY FIRE
#16 NEVER SAY DIE
#17 STAY TUNED FOR DANGER
#18 CIRCLE OF EVIL
#19 SISTERS IN CRIME
#20 VERY DEADLY YOURS
#21 RECIPE FOR MURDER
#22 FATAL ATTRACTION
#23 SINISTER PARADISE
#24 TILL DEATH DO US PART
#25 RICH AND DANGEROUS
#26 PLAYING WITH FIRE
#27 MOST LIKELY TO DIE
#28 THE BLACK WIDOW
#29 PURE POISON
#30 DEATH BY DESIGN
#31 TROUBLE IN TAHITI
#32 HIGH MARKS FOR MALICE
#33 DANGER IN DISGUISE
#34 VANISHING ACT
#35 BAD MEDICINE
#36 OVER THE EDGE
#37 LAST DANCE
#38 THE FINAL SCENE
#39 THE SUSPECT NEXT DOOR
#40 SHADOW OF A DOUBT
#41 SOMETHING TO HIDE
#42 THE WRONG CHEMISTRY

Available from ARCHWAY Paperbacks

THE WRONG CHEMISTRY

Carolyn Keene

AN ARCHWAY PAPERBACK
Published by POCKET BOOKS
New York London Toronto Sydney Tokyo

AN ARCHWAY PAPERBACK *Original*

An Archway Paperback published by
POCKET BOOKS, a division of Simon & Schuster Inc.
1230 Avenue of the Americas, New York, NY 10020

Produced by Mega-Books of New York, Inc.

ISBN: 0-671-67494-3

First Archway Paperback printing December 1989

10 9 8 7 6 5 4 3 2 1

Printed in the U.S.A.

IL 7+

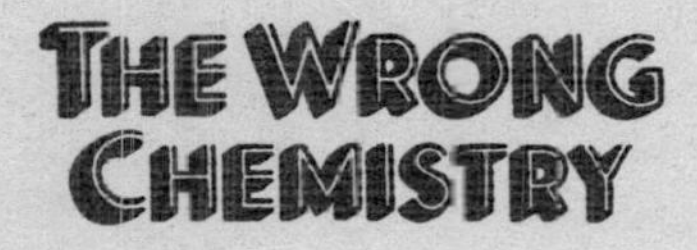
THE WRONG
CHEMISTRY

Chapter One

"YOU'RE NANCY DREW—the detective?" Dean William Jarvis blurted out. "I thought you'd be, well, older." The dean, a bear of a man wearing a tweedy brown suit, paused halfway between sitting and standing to stare at the slim young woman in front of him.

Nancy grinned and pushed back a strand of reddish blond hair. "I *am* only eighteen, but it's easier to go undercover as a college student when you look like one." She extended her hand to the dean, and he took it, looking somewhat sheepish.

"I didn't mean to insult you," the dean said quickly.

"That's okay," Nancy continued. "I should apologize for wearing jeans to our meeting, but it's a long drive from River Heights to Emerson College. You can't beat jeans for comfort."

The dean's round face reddened, and he gestured for Nancy to sit down. "No apologies, please. Excuse my rudeness. I know you're a top-notch detective, and that's all that matters. Pat Burnett, our basketball coach, told me how great you were at finding the prankster who was harassing his team. I'm just nervous and about at my wit's end."

Nancy settled into an overstuffed chair next to the dean's desk. She purposely kept her tone light and casual. The dean was alarmed. Besides, she'd get more information from him if she acted totally together.

"You mentioned a theft and the need for secrecy on the telephone last night. Can you give me any details?"

The dean leaned forward, touching his fingertips together nervously. He gave her a helpless smile. "That's part of the problem. I can't give you details. This involves the government—and it's all very hush-hush and top secret."

Nancy drew back, startled. "Top secret?"

Dean Jarvis had been very abrupt when he called her the night before and asked her if she could come to Emerson immediately. Nancy had been planning a short vacation with her friends Bess and George but had leapt at a chance to work at the college instead. Nancy's boyfriend, Ned Nickerson, was a student at Emerson, and Nancy hadn't seen him for ages.

Now, looking at the worry lines in the dean's face, Nancy knew she'd have to think of Ned second. Reaching into her brown leather purse, she pulled out a notepad and pen.

"You don't have to tell me government secrets," she assured the dean. "But I'll need to know all the facts that you can tell."

"Are you ready? It's a long story." Dean Jarvis smiled and took a deep breath. "Emerson is host to a visiting professor, Josef Maszak. Maszak is working on a top secret experiment sponsored by the U.S. government. You *do* know what a visiting professor is, don't you?"

"Someone who's on campus for only a semester or two?" Nancy suggested.

"Yes, usually. But this is a little different. Our government is running a special visiting-professor program involving scientists only. Each one is a specialist working on a secret government experiment. It's considered a great honor to have one of these scientists placed at your school."

"I'm sure you're proud that Emerson was chosen," Nancy said politely.

"Very," the dean agreed eagerly. "We worked five years to qualify. We had to expand our entire science program. This project is important to me—I won't let it fail."

"No," Nancy said, careful to keep her comments neutral.

"I can't tell you much about what Maszak does," the dean said, "because it's secret and because those parts I can share are far too technical. But twice a month, the government sends him a quantity of a substance called CLT. It's a rare chemical, and the government monitors it closely."

The dean anxiously ran his fingers through his hair. "Twice now, just as Maszak reached a crucial stage of his experiment, someone has broken into his lab and stolen the CLT."

"Is CLT dangerous?" Nancy asked.

"Maszak says no," the dean responded. "He swears there's no known use for CLT, except for his experiment. But it is a rare chemical, so he keeps it under lock and key. I tell you, Ms. Drew, I never dreamed it would be stolen."

"Useless," Nancy repeated thoughtfully. "But someone went to a lot of trouble to steal it." Nancy quickly went on. "Who knows about the thefts?"

"No one." The dean's voice dropped to a whisper. "I haven't reported either of them to the government yet," he admitted. "The first time the CLT was taken, I decided it was some kind of a prank. I thought whoever took it might return it. I admit it, Ms. Drew, I was afraid. Afraid that if I reported the theft, the government would order Maszak to leave. Emerson would be disgraced, our reputation ruined. But after the second theft . . ." His voice trailed off.

Nancy's eyes narrowed. "I'm not sure I like keeping secrets from the government."

The dean looked flustered. "Ms. Drew—Nancy—please help me. Help Emerson. I'm sorry I can't tell you more. If you can't take the case, I'll understand, but I'm asking you to try."

"I *could* use more information," Nancy said, feeling frustrated.

"I'll make a deal with you," the dean said. "Try to find the thief. If you fail, I'll call in the government. But not just yet. Losing Maszak now would be a blow Emerson might never recover from."

Nancy hesitated. "Dean Jarvis," she finally asked, "if I did agree to take the case, could I trust Maszak?"

"Absolutely," the dean swore. "Maszak's an honest man, a truly dedicated scientist . . ." The dean's voice trailed off as he looked directly at Nancy. "At least that's what I used to think," he said slowly. "I guess I don't really know anymore. At this point, I'm not sure whom to believe or whom to trust."

Nancy saw a look of confusion pass over the dean's eyes. "It makes no sense!" he exclaimed. "The lab is constantly locked. The CLT is in an inner lab, sealed by another lock, which also has an alarm. The security guard on that floor gives me the security logs to check each day. Only Professor Maszak and his assistant are even allowed near the CLT, and they all have government clearance."

"And yet," Nancy said thoughtfully, "the CLT has been stolen twice, and the thief knows exactly when to take it. Every sign points to an inside job. But from what you've told me, it *can't* be an inside job."

The dean got up, walked around, and perched on the edge of his desk so he was closer to Nancy. "This sounds impossible, I know, but what we have here is an impossible crime."

Nancy stood up, too. "I'll need as much information as you can get me on Professor Maszak and his assistant," she said briskly.

"I'm sure I can find something in the files." Dean Jarvis sounded hopeful for the first time. "Does this mean you'll take the case?"

Nancy grinned in return. "I may be young, Dean Jarvis, but I am experienced. And the one thing I've learned as a detective is that there *is* no such thing as an impossible crime."

The dean looked pleased. "You do inspire confidence. I can't thank you enough, Nancy."

"Don't thank me until I've solved the case," Nancy said. "Well, I guess we're done for now. I'd like to see Professor Maszak's lab this afternoon, if that can be arranged."

"Professor Maszak already knows about you. I'll tell him you'll be stopping by. As for going undercover, you'll need a story and a place to stay. I've made arrangements for you to take an empty room in one of the dorms. Holland, I believe it is. We'll say you're a transfer student. You're going to work on the school newspaper, and you're writing a story on Professor Maszak. If anyone checks on you, my office will be able to back up your story."

"Good," Nancy said approvingly. "I'll be able to ask as many questions as I need!" She glanced at her watch. "I'll have to start right after lunch."

"Let me take you to your dorm," Dean Jarvis offered.

Nancy colored slightly. "Actually, Dean, I'm late for a lunch date—with my boyfriend."

The dean beamed at her. "Ned Nickerson, right? A star athlete in both football and basketball—a nice young man."

"Yes, he is," Nancy said. Nancy had a vision

of her tall, handsome boyfriend pacing his fraternity living room waiting for her. She hadn't seen him in almost a month. Her heart had raced when she realized that because of this case they would have some time together.

Nancy flipped her notebook closed and slipped it back in her purse. "Can you tell me the quickest way to Omega Chi Epsilon from here?" Omega Chi was Ned's fraternity.

"There's a shortcut no one ever uses," Dean Jarvis said. "Go straight down the main road, and take your second right. I'll send whatever information we have on Maszak and his assistant to the dorm for you."

"Thanks." Nancy scooped up her purse.

Outside the administration building, a chill wind was attempting to dislodge autumn leaves from their branches. It had rained while Nancy was inside, and the ground was slick with wet leaves. Shivering, she zipped up her soft suede jacket and slipped on her sunglasses to protect her eyes from the afternoon sun. She climbed back into her Mustang, flipped on the tape deck, and headed for Ned's fraternity house.

Emerson was a large college with lots of trees and wide-open spaces. The road the dean had recommended was narrow and looked deserted as it wound through the campus arboretum. Nancy enjoyed handling the Mustang around the road's many curves.

As she came around an especially tight turn, Nancy saw a dull green shape lying in the road just ahead. Instantly she stepped on the brakes, her heart thumping. The car screeched to a halt, only inches from the lifeless body of a young man.

Chapter Two

Her heart in her throat, Nancy scanned the accident scene. Her mind, trained by detective work, was already racing. Was the boy the victim of a hit-and-run accident? No. No other cars were in sight. She saw no fresh tire tracks on the road to indicate a skid or sudden stop. Leaping out of her car, Nancy ran to the young man, who was dressed in army camouflage clothes.

"Are you all right?" she asked. "Can you hear me?"

No answer. Nancy crouched down to take the boy's pulse. She just had time to register how strong it was when she heard a voice behind her.

"Don't touch him, and don't make a move."

Nancy whirled around and was now facing another young man in army camouflage. Only he was holding a gun and had it pointed right at her.

Nancy gasped. The newcomer was thin and wore wire-rimmed glasses. Without the gun, he would have looked harmless. But Nancy wasn't making any assumptions, not while the boy had a gun trained on her.

Nancy eyed him uneasily as she slowly got to her feet, her hands up. More people emerged from between the trees.

"Hey, Peter, cut the kidding," a female voice called. A girl with long blond hair jogged easily toward them.

Sheepishly, the boy lowered his gun, giving Nancy an embarrassed smile. "It's not real," he muttered. He walked over to the body on the ground and nudged it gently with his foot. "You better get up, Bob. Here comes Karen."

The blond girl, Karen, reached them just then, glaring at both boys. She was tiny, Nancy realized—she barely came up to Nancy's chin.

"Hi," she said in a breathless voice. She gave Nancy a warm smile. "Sorry—these guys are idiots. Bob, get up!" she ordered furiously, as the "body" jumped to his feet. She turned back to Nancy and offered her the young man's gun. "See, it's a toy, really. A fancy water pistol."

"Water pistol or not," Nancy said in measured tones, "I don't like any gun pointed at my head. And Bob should be more careful," she added. "I could have run into him for real."

Karen flushed and pushed her hair back nervously. Nancy noticed a large, bronze-colored earring shaped like a snake on her right ear.

"Everybody, take a break," she yelled to the small group who had gathered a few yards away, watching them. She turned to Nancy, concern in her clear blue eyes.

"I'm Karen Lewis," she said, "and we're just, um, rehearsing for an event we're staging this week. I think Pete and Bob were trying to see if someone would take them seriously. I'm really sorry. They just got carried away."

Relief and anger coursed through Nancy. "Well," she said, drawing in a long breath, "I guess I've had worse scares."

"Are you a student here?"

"Yes. That is, a new student. I just transferred. My name is Nancy Drew."

Karen groaned. "Oh, no, someone new. Listen, you won't report us, will you?"

"Why would I do that?" Nancy asked. "What exactly is going on here?"

Without replying, Karen turned and searched

the group around her. "Philip!" she called anxiously.

A swarthy man got up from the rock he was sitting on and sauntered toward them. Unlike the others, he wasn't wearing camouflage clothes. Instead, he had on jeans, a black leather jacket, black sneakers, and a white scarf wrapped a little too casually around his neck. A shock of white hair stood out in the wavy black hair that tumbled over his head. He was too old to be a student, but he looked more like a model than a college professor, Nancy thought.

"A problem, Karen?" he asked in a low voice. He wasn't particularly large or stocky, but in the group of students, his presence seemed overwhelming.

"I hope not," she said, eyeing Nancy. "This is Nancy Drew, she's a transfer student."

"Nice to meet you, Nancy. I'm Philip Bangs." Turning his black eyes toward Nancy, he held out his hand, grasping hers with confidence. "Is there some trouble?"

"Suppose you tell me," Nancy said, trying to hide the curiosity in her voice. This was more than a group of overgrown kids playing with water pistols, or Karen wouldn't be so nervous.

Karen turned to Bangs and lowered her voice. "Well . . ." She hesitated. "I never got a permit to use the arboretum. If complaint charges are filed, the dean might kick us off campus."

Nancy cut in, a little irritated with the way Karen acted as if she weren't there. "I'm sure Dean Jarvis has more important things to worry about than permits. Who are you, anyway, some kind of officers-in-training group?"

Philip Bangs gave her a wide, startling smile. "Officers in training!" he exclaimed, as if it were an extremely clever joke. He clapped Karen on the shoulder, and the girl seemed to relax.

"No, we're not part of any army," Bangs said, chuckling lightly. "But we are part of a group. Members of POE—Protect Our Environment. Maybe you've heard of us? You might be interested in joining our group. I have some flyers here. We were merely preparing for Senator Claiborne's visit." Bangs began to dig through his jacket pockets.

"Maybe later, thanks," Nancy said firmly. "I'm late for an appointment. And you don't have to worry about me—I'm not going to file any charges against anyone. It's not my style." Flashing what she hoped was a convincing smile, Nancy climbed back into her car.

The last thing she needed was to get involved with an organized group, no matter how noble their cause. Not when she had a mystery to solve.

As Nancy pulled up in front of Omega Chi Epsilon she spotted Ned instantly. He was sitting on the wide porch, his long, jean-clad legs stretched out in front of him. She was really late, she realized, looking at her watch. Ned jumped lightly to his feet and headed toward her.

"Hey, gorgeous!" he said, waiting for her to climb out so he could enfold her in his arms. "Welcome back to Emerson!"

"Ned!" Nancy hugged him tightly with her eyes closed, breathing in his warm, familiar smell. "I missed you."

"Mmm," he murmured, "I missed you, too." He tilted her head up, his dark eyes dancing. "Give me a kiss."

Nancy leaned back against the car, letting her body relax next to Ned's. This was the kind of welcome she liked!

After a moment Nancy broke away, laughing. "Ned, don't you think we should go inside?"

"And get more comfortable?" he teased, keeping an arm around her waist. Nancy slipped her arm around him, her head fitting perfectly in the hollow of his shoulder, as they strolled toward the frat house.

A crackling fire greeted Nancy as she entered the living room, which was comfortably furnished with overstuffed chairs and sofas. Ned guided her to a sofa in front of the fire.

"Nan, you remember Jan and Mike."

Jan Teller, a small brunette, bounced up and embraced Nancy quickly. "It's great to see you again," she said warmly.

"Ditto for me," Mike O'Shea said. "Don't mind if I don't get up." Mike gestured to the cane lying next to him on the floor. "Jan and I just had a walk. I made it all the way to the gym and back. I'm going to claim invalid's privileges and make *you* come to *me.*"

Grinning, Nancy leaned over and gave Mike a peck on the cheek. He grabbed her hand. "Thanks again for everything you did last time you were here. I know it was pretty rough on you, but you brought me to my senses."

Nancy had met Mike and Jan when she came to Emerson to try to find a practical joker who was ruining Emerson's chance at a basketball championship. Mike had been Nancy's number-one suspect.

Nancy shuddered, remembering the case. Mike *had* been involved, but when Nancy had confronted him, he'd realized his mistakes and tried to put an end to his part in it. Eventually, Nancy did find the real criminal, but not before he'd pushed Mike off a six-story building.

Ned squeezed Nancy's shoulder, drawing her closer to him. She could tell he was thinking about that case, too. Ned had been so upset by what happened to Mike that he and Nancy had broken up for a while. But they solved their problems, Nancy thought thankfully, and they were together again, stronger than ever.

"How are you doing?" Nancy asked Mike.

"Okay." He shrugged. "My back injuries weren't as bad as the doctors first thought, and my leg is healing. I can even walk short distances now without the cane."

"I'm going to rummage around for some chips or something. Anyone want anything?" Jan headed for the kitchen.

"Yeah, bring everything you can carry," Ned called. "I'm starving!"

"Ned, I'm sorry," Nancy said in dismay. "You should have gone to lunch without me."

"And missed my number-one girl? No way! But we will have dinner tonight—at a very romantic little place I know," Ned said. "But what did happen? Did Dean Jarvis keep you talking? I know he loves to talk."

"Partly, but then I ran into some people," Nancy said wryly. "Literally. Do you know about POE?"

Ned groaned. "Not them. Did they try to recruit you?"

"Sort of." Nancy explained what happened in the arboretum.

"Water guns? They're nuts!" Ned exclaimed. "They might mean well, but their methods—" He shuddered.

"Ned's right," Mike agreed. "I'm all for protecting the environment, but I think there are better ways to do it. POE's tactics are weird."

"What exactly do they do?" Nancy asked.

"They go out in the woods where they live off the land and go rock climbing and stuff. And they're always talking about stopping any technology that threatens the environment," Ned said in a steely voice.

Nancy frowned. "Well, those all sound like good causes."

"They *are* good causes," Jan said lightly, coming back in the room. "Ned's exaggerating. Right now they're all fired up about a visit from Senator Claiborne."

"I read about that," Nancy exclaimed. "He's the one who thinks we should sell our national parklands to developers. Most people think he's a genuine nut. If POE is against him, I'll have to be for them."

Jan and Mike exchanged uneasy looks. Nancy noticed Ned's jaw clench and anger wash over his face.

"Did I say something wrong?" she asked warily. She started to put her hand on Ned's shoulder, but he backed away. Nancy felt her heart sink.

"Maybe we should stop all this talking and eat," Nancy said, trying to change the subject. "It's not too late for this snack, is it?"

Ned glanced at his watch. "I'm afraid it is,"

he said curtly. "Anyway, I don't have much appetite now, and we're going to be late for class. Come on, Mike, Jan. We've got to hurry."

Jan helped Mike to his feet. Giving Nancy apologetic looks, they headed for the front door.

"Ned, what's wrong?" Nancy grabbed Ned's arm as he started to follow Jan and Mike out of the room. "A minute ago you were so happy to see me. What happened? What did I do?"

Ned pulled away. At the front door he stopped, his face set in a hard mask. Nancy stared, completely baffled by the change in him.

"If you think POE is such a great group, fine. But just do me a favor, okay? Don't ever mention them in front of me again!"

Chapter Three

NANCY WAS STUNNED. She'd been so thrilled to see Ned, and now this. It was so unlike him to overreact. Whatever she did, Nancy vowed, she wouldn't mention POE.

She watched as Ned walked off with Jan and Mike. As soon as he had calmed down, she'd find out why her sticking up for the group had upset him so much. But there wasn't anything she could do about it now, so she decided to find her dorm and unpack.

Nancy didn't have to share her room, and it had a private bath. With a sigh, she dumped her bags, plopped onto the bed, and kicked off her shoes. Then she remembered she had promised to let her father, Carson Drew, know when she had arrived.

Rolling onto her stomach, Nancy grabbed the phone and dialed. Her father's voice came over the wire.

"Carson Drew," he answered pleasantly.

"Hi, Dad. Just called to let you know I'm safe and sound."

"I knew you would be, but it's always nice to hear your voice. Have you learned anything more about the case yet?"

Carson Drew was a celebrated lawyer, and he was always interested in Nancy's cases. The famous father had passed his curiosity on to his daughter, and it was one of the things that made her such a good detective.

"It's pretty fascinating," Nancy began. She stopped, having heard a noise in the hall. "Hold on, Dad. Someone's at the door. The dean promised to send over some information, and this is probably it."

Nancy tucked the telephone under her chin and went to the door, dragging the long cord behind her. Before she could open the door, an envelope was slid under it.

Stooping, Nancy quickly grabbed the envelope and opened the door just in time to see the back of the person who had obviously delivered it.

"Hey, thanks," she called.

Whoever it was gave a casual wave but didn't turn around or slow down to look back.

"Oh, well," Nancy said to her father, explaining what had just happened. "So much for the natives being friendly." The envelope was much smaller than Nancy had expected. Puzzled, she weighed it in her hand. Judging from the envelope's lightness, there wasn't much information on Professor Maszak at all.

Shrugging, she slit open the flap and gave her father a brief account of her conversation with the dean. She described how secretive Professor Maszak's experiment was, and how difficult it would make her investigation.

"That *is* a problem," Carson said sympathetically. "But maybe this new information will help you out."

"Maybe," Nancy agreed. She pulled a piece of paper out of the envelope and scanned it quickly.

"Nan?" her father asked after a long silence. "Are you still there?"

"Uh—sorry, Dad." Nancy shook herself. "It's—well, there isn't much information here after all."

"Looks like you have your work cut out for you," Nancy heard her father say. "But that's nothing new."

"I guess not," Nancy answered, smiling wryly. "Look, Dad, I've got to go. It looks like this case is going to be harder than I thought."

Hanging up, Nancy stared at the piece of paper in her hand. She hadn't wanted to worry her father, but the envelope wasn't from Dean Jarvis.

Instead, it was a warning, hastily scrawled in bold red ink. "Go home, Nancy Drew. CLT is *not* in your future."

Nancy quickly ran back into the hall, but there was no sign of the messenger who'd delivered the threat. Making her way down to the lounge, she tried to remember what the person had looked like.

She questioned the girl at the front desk, but she hadn't seen anyone who matched the sketchy description Nancy gave either enter or leave the building. In fact, the look the girl gave Nancy as she questioned her made her blush.

"Listen, if you remember anything, let me know. You can leave a note at the desk," Nancy said.

"Sure," the girl said, rolling her eyes.

It wasn't the best start to an investigation. Already, just minutes into the case, Nancy had missed an important clue by not paying attention to what was happening around her. It wouldn't happen again.

She had to admit that part of her mind was still on Ned. Why had he been so angry with her earlier? Well, if she couldn't figure Ned out, at least she could track down the missing CLT.

Squaring her shoulders, she set off for the science labs a quarter mile away toward the center of the campus. A steady stream of students poured from the building entrance, jostling and shouting, obviously in high spirits at the end of the day. Nancy waded through them to the big glass double doors.

An unattended desk stood on one side of the almost deserted lobby. Pausing at the elevator banks, Nancy checked the directory. Professor Maszak's lab was on the third floor.

When the elevator doors opened on the third floor, Nancy found herself face-to-face with a security guard seated behind a desk.

"Signature and ID," he said automatically, without looking up from his magazine. "But classes are over for the day."

"I'm not here for class," she replied to the brim of his cap. "And I don't have an ID. I'm here to see Professor Josef Maszak."

The guard glanced up sharply. "What did you say your name was?"

He reached for the sheet she had just signed. "Nancy Drew. Wait a minute." The guard checked another piece of paper. "Right—you've got clearance." Then he went back to reading. "Last door on your right," he mumbled.

Nancy raised her eyebrows. Some security! The guard hadn't even tried to verify who she was. It obviously wasn't very difficult for anyone to get into the building. She hoped the lab itself was better protected.

Nancy found the door easily and knocked.

"It's open," someone called.

Great security, Nancy thought again as she entered a large, bright room dominated by huge picture windows. Long lab desks, each with a sink and gas outlets, faced the chalkboard in the front of the room. Three or four students were still there, bent over the tables.

"Excuse me," Nancy ventured. "Is Professor Maszak here?"

A freckle-faced boy gestured to a door on his left. A large combination lock was mounted on the wall next to it, but the door was slightly ajar.

"Right there, in his office," the boy said.

Nancy pushed into a much smaller room strewn with lab equipment. Professor Maszak sat on a high stool behind a counter busily doing paperwork. His bush of salt-and-pepper hair obscured his face.

"You're late," he barked.

"I didn't know I was expected," Nancy said pleasantly.

The professor started. He raised his head, his light brown eyes widening in alarm. Color rushed into his face.

"Who do you think you are, sneaking up on me like that? How did you get in here?"

"It wasn't very hard," Nancy said pointedly. "Dean Jarvis said this room was always under lock and key."

Maszak had the grace to look embarrassed. "I left it open only for a minute," he said, defending himself. "I was expecting my assistant, Sara," he muttered. "I thought you were she."

"I'm Nancy Drew."

"Oh, now I remember. I *was* expecting you," the fiftyish Maszak said gruffly.

He got up, wiping his hands on a dirty lab coat, and closed the door. "Jarvis told me he'd called you in to investigate." He eyed Nancy closely. "You don't look much like a famous detective."

Nancy ignored the remark and surveyed the room. A ten-foot fish tank ran along the right wall and several open-wire cages covered the left. An industrial-size freezer filled the back of the room. Maszak motioned Nancy over to the fish tank.

"This," he announced proudly, "is my experiment."

The tank held carp of all sizes, but one very large fish swam along the bottom of the tank. Nancy bent closer. The fish was enormous.

Professor Maszak's eyes followed hers. "My

pride and joy," he said. "How old do you think he is?"

Nancy had no idea how to judge the age of a fish. "A year?" she guessed.

Maszak snorted. "Six months," he said proudly. "Can you believe it?"

Smiling slightly, Nancy went to examine the cages. Each one held several mice, which ranged from normal size to several exceptionally large ones.

"I take it CLT is some kind of growth drug," she remarked.

"You're very quick," the professor said. "That's precisely what it is."

Nancy stared at him. What kind of "top secret" experiment was this? First, there was hardly any security around the lab, and then the professor practically boasted about his so-called secret experiment.

"I don't understand," Nancy told him. "I thought this was all restricted information. It can't be as simple as a chemical to grow bigger fish and mice."

Maszak laughed. "Some people get a little carried away with the cloak-and-dagger stuff," he said, returning to his papers and shuffling them. "CLT is a rare, extremely expensive chemical. There are others that give much the same results."

"And it isn't dangerous?" Nancy asked, feeling more and more confused.

The professor snorted. "If you drink it, it'll give you a stomachache. But if you mean, is it potentially lethal, the answer is no."

"The dean told me that both times the CLT was stolen, it was taken at a very crucial time during your experiment."

"Well, yes," Maszak said, "but not during the experiment, *before* it. I treat the CLT in a special way that only I have the formula for. It's a lengthy process. After it's treated, I put the finished product in the freezer. That was when the CLT was stolen."

Maszak threw open the freezer door. On the lower shelf, Nancy saw a large metal cylinder that nearly filled the freezer.

Nancy whistled in surprise. "It's huge! I guess I thought they'd be smaller."

"The amounts are very small," Maszak explained. "The CLT itself is sealed in small plastic tubes. The container helps keep it at the right temperature. I got a canister in this delivery," he continued. "My first delivery was two canisters, and one of them was stolen. My second delivery was only one canister and it was stolen. But I did do work with the one canister that wasn't stolen."

"And now you're about to complete the third treatment?" Nancy asked.

Maszak eyed her with grudging admiration. "As you guessed," he said, gesturing to a mass of test tubes set up at the other counter from where he had been doing his paperwork, "I'm in the final stages of treatment now."

Nancy examined the tubes and beakers on the central counter. They meant nothing to her. Maszak could be telling the truth, or giving her the runaround to hide his real purpose. Without some hard facts about the experiment, there was no way for her to know for sure.

A noise came from the outer lab. Frowning, Maszak hurried to the door. Nancy followed him.

The students she'd seen before had left the lab, but in their place was a girl with brown hair who was standing at a lab table near the windows. She was holding a beaker up to the light. Her scarf and bag had been thrown over a nearby chair, but she still had her coat on.

"You're late again, Sara!" Maszak exclaimed. "Nancy, this is my assistant, Sara Hughes."

As the girl whirled around, a look of fear flashed across her plump face.

"I—I know I'm late," she stuttered, "but I can finish this up in a minute."

Maszak nodded curtly. "Nancy is here to interview me for the paper. She may want to ask you some questions, too."

The girl looked guardedly at Nancy. "Well, I

have to get this done right away. I don't have time for questions."

Sara turned back to the setup on the table and gently scooped some dull gray powder into a small measuring spoon.

"At least take off your coat," Maszak said.

Still balancing the spoon in her right hand, Sara began to unbutton her coat with her left hand. She shrugged her shoulders vigorously, trying to slip the coat off.

"Sara, watch yourself," Maszak cautioned. "Remember what you've got in your hands!"

Nancy had an impulse to help, but as she came up behind Sara, the girl suddenly twisted sharply, then stumbled. As she reached to steady herself, the spoon fell from her hand. The gray powder landed in the beaker with a small fizz.

"Watch out!" Maszak cried.

The beaker exploded, sending splinters of glass flying everywhere!

Chapter Four

CLOSING HER EYES, Nancy threw up her hands to cover her face. She heard Professor Maszak yell to Sara to protect herself as pieces of glass clattered to the floor. Sara gave a little cry, and Nancy heard her footsteps as she rushed out of the room.

When Nancy opened her eyes, the professor was staring after Sara with a rueful expression. He bent to pick up the larger fragments from the floor.

Nancy bent down to help him. "What *was* that?" she asked.

Maszak sighed. "Nothing. A stupid mistake."

Nancy arched an eyebrow.

"Sara is supervising two class experiments at once. She wasn't paying attention, and she dropped part of one into part of the other. They didn't agree with each other."

"To put it mildly," Nancy murmured. "Shouldn't she take better precautions with explosives?"

"Neither is explosive by itself. The powder is zinc," the professor said. "And there was hydrochloric acid in the beaker." The professor was silent for a moment, studying the glass fragments nestled in his palm. "But you're right. They shouldn't have been near each other. I'm afraid Sara has been a little distracted lately. I'll have to speak to her about it." He didn't seem to be looking forward to their conversation.

"I have to get ready for a dinner date," Nancy told him, hoping Ned was still speaking to her. "But if I need to ask any more questions, where can I reach you?"

"Here or at home. I live in Adams Cottage, near the main gate. But I'm usually here."

Nancy thanked the professor and left the lab. She decided to head back to the dorm to see if Dean Jarvis had sent the information he'd promised or to check if Ned called. Nothing. She'd have to check with both of them later.

Nancy flopped on her bed and tried to concentrate on the case, but her thoughts kept coming back to Ned. She hated it when they fought, especially when there wasn't any real reason for it. She decided then and there to do whatever it took to make up with Ned.

After a quick shower, Nancy slipped on her blue silk dress—Ned's favorite. In that dress she could smooth out their problems. The soft fabric flowed smoothly over her hips. She brushed back her thick hair, which looked more gold than red in the artificial light, and was just running some clear gloss over her lips when the telephone rang. Nancy's heart leapt.

"Nancy, this is Mike O'Shea. I hope I didn't disturb you."

"No, not at all." Nancy swallowed her disappointment. She'd have to call Ned as soon as Mike hung up. "What's up?"

"Well," Mike said, hesitating, "it's Ned. He ran out of here an hour ago, on his way to the dining hall. He said it was an emergency and asked me to let you know where he was if he wasn't back by now."

So much for the dress! Nancy thought. "Thanks, Mike," she said into the phone. "I'll look for him in the dining hall right away."

What kind of emergency? Nancy wondered as she found her way to the campus dining hall. A steady stream of students walked in and out of the modern glass-and-chrome building. Inside the cafeteria, each student shouted to be heard over rock music blaring through loudspeakers.

Nancy spotted Ned sitting at a table in the corner, his face bent close to a thin, dark-haired girl next to him. One tray of mostly eaten food sat between them. Nancy was happy to see Ned was wearing a coat and tie. Maybe she could salvage their dinner plans after all.

Ned looked startled as Nancy reached their table. Undaunted, she slipped into a chair and put her hand on his arm.

"Nan, I didn't really mean for you to come over here. But . . ." Ned gave her a brief, although distracted, smile and turned back to the other girl.

"Angela Morrow, this is Nancy Drew."

Angela's face was pale against her jet black hair. As she swung her head to greet Nancy a single bronze earring in the shape of a snake slapped gently against her neck. It was the same kind of earring Karen Lewis had been wearing, Nancy noted.

Angela was nervously twisting a piece of paper.

"Excuse me, Angela," Nancy said, "but that earring—are you a member of . . ." Her voice trailed away as Ned shot her a warning look.

"Nancy met some members of POE today," Ned told Angela softly. "She ran into them in the arboretum behind my frat house." Ned turned to Nancy. "Angela's going to be initiated into the group tonight. I'm trying to talk her out of it."

"Ned!" Angela's voice was surprisingly soft. "I've told you, POE is a wonderful organization, a community of people working together to protect our planet. Why is that so hard for you to understand?"

"Angela, look." Ned's voice matched the exasperation in Angela's, and Nancy sensed they had had this conversation before. "I don't trust POE, no matter what you say. Some students in the group are moving off campus to live together in a commune. They've stopped going to classes. They spend all their time in private meetings at POE headquarters, and there's something secretive and nasty about the whole thing."

Angela appealed to Nancy. "We do a lot of good," she insisted. "We have great speakers come to campus—reputable people. And we have a tremendous recruiting effort."

"My point exactly! If it's such a great group, why do you have to work so hard to recruit new members?"

Nancy looked at Ned in surprise. She realized he was genuinely worried about Angela's safety, but he was making her feel very awkward—as if he cared more about Angela than about Nancy herself. Embarrassed by her jealousy, she tried to be more reasonable. There was nothing wrong with Ned having Angela for a friend.

"Ned," she began uncomfortably, "I know you feel strongly about this, but Angela has a right to do what she wants."

Ned glared at her angrily. "I have nothing against free speech, or the right to peaceful protest," he snapped.

Nancy felt helpless. "Have you been to many of their meetings?" she asked.

"Never!" Angela fumed. "He hasn't been to a single one, but he thinks he knows what it's all about!"

"The meetings are useless," Ned argued. "You can only find out what's really going on if you're initiated."

Nancy shrugged helplessly. "Then Angela *should* be initiated. If there's anything wrong with the group, she can find out before getting more involved."

Ned's eyes narrowed. "Right. But what if, once you're initiated, you don't like what you find out?" His voice dropped. "I've never heard of anyone quitting," he warned.

Angela rolled her eyes impatiently. Nancy squirmed self-consciously in her seat. She picked up a book of matches from the glass ashtray. On the cover was an ad for Reiko's, the Japanese restaurant she was hoping Ned would take her to. It didn't seem likely now. Sighing, she slipped the matches into her purse.

"I give up," Angela exclaimed. "Try talking to someone else. Like Philip Bangs. He came to speak to us today. He's a world-famous environmentalist. You'd believe him, wouldn't you?"

Philip Bangs—the man in black in the woods. Nancy felt Angela staring at her curiously.

"I—I met Mr. Bangs today," she explained. "He was quite impressive."

Angela beamed in triumph. "There! Nancy believes me. Bangs is terrific. He studied to be a doctor and is also a computer specialist. He has the medical and scientific training to know what technology is dangerous. He's really inspiring."

Ned growled in disgust, but Angela nodded eagerly at Nancy. "He traveled all over the world and finally settled in South America. But he felt a great need to help people, so he came back to America."

"Angela," Nancy interrupted, "when I met Bangs today he was with a group in the arboretum, playing some kind of game with water guns. He said it had to do with Senator Claiborne coming. Do you know what that was all about?"

Angela lowered her eyes, and for the first time she looked slightly uncomfortable. "POE is going to protest Claiborne's views on national parklands."

"With water pistols?" Ned snorted. "Are you planning to drown him?"

Nancy hid a smile.

"Are you a student here?" Angela asked abruptly.

Nancy didn't blame Angela for trying to change the subject. She'd never seen Ned acting so unreasonably.

"Yes, I recently transferred here," she began, but Ned cut her off.

"Angela," he pleaded, "I'm sorry if I'm acting crazy. I'm worried. Can't we talk about this some more?" He smiled. "I even promise to listen with an open mind."

Angela pushed her chair back and got up. "There's nothing more to talk about," she said lightly, giving Ned a quick peck on the cheek. Then she turned to Nancy. "Nice meeting you. If you want to know any more about POE, just give me a call."

"Angela, wait," Ned said, standing up. "Let me walk you back to your dorm." He turned to Nancy. "Nan? Do you mind? About dinner, I mean."

"No, I guess not," Nancy said.

Relief flooded Ned's face. "I'll call you later. We can have dessert or something," he promised vaguely.

Disappointed and upset, Nancy watched them go. It certainly wasn't the evening she'd had in mind. What was Ned's problem with POE anyway? Why was he getting so upset about a simple college group? There had to be something he wasn't telling her, and Nancy resolved that she was going to find out what it was.

Leaving the cafeteria, Nancy impulsively turned toward the lab. The streetlights cast friendly circles of light in the cold darkness that turned Nancy's breath into puffs of white fog. She turned up her collar to give her ears some protection and dug into her pockets for her leather gloves.

Usually, she thought ruefully, something ruined her time with Ned when she was on a case, but usually it was her fault, not his.

Nancy made out the silhouette of the science building against the sky. Counting the stories, she realized there was a light shining on the third floor. As she watched, someone passed in front of the lab's huge windows. Even from a distance, she thought she recognized the figure. Sara Hughes?

Quickening her pace, Nancy hurried to the lab. If Sara was alone, now was the perfect opportunity to ask the skittish lab assistant some pointed questions about Maszak, his experiments, and CLT.

As she approached the front steps of the building, Nancy heard the distinctive sound of a twig breaking behind her.

From the corner of her eye, she saw a low branch of a nearby tree swaying gently. Probably an owl or raccoon, Nancy thought, not fully convinced. Before she took another full step a hand came down heavily on her shoulder, and before she could turn around, something crashed over her head. Everything went black.

Chapter Five

"Can you hear me, Nan? Are you okay?"

Nancy opened her eyes to find herself lying in bed in a room flooded with morning light. Ned's face was close to hers, his soft brown eyes full of concern. Her head ached terribly.

"I—I think so," Nancy said weakly. She put a hand to her throbbing forehead. "Except for this headache. Where am I?"

"In the infirmary. What happened to you?"

"Can I tell you as soon as my head clears and I see less than three of you?" Nancy asked.

Ned nodded and took her hand gently. "I'm glad you're awake."

Seeing the warmth in Ned's eyes, Nancy was overcome with relief. She pulled herself up, threw her arms around his neck, and held him tight. Wordlessly, he brushed his lips against her forehead.

"Oh, Ned," she whispered. "What's going on with us? I thought you hated me."

"Hated you? Never! I was so worried about Angela that I got carried away. It's all my fault."

"I'm sorry—" Nancy began.

"Shhh." Ned placed his fingers gently over Nancy's lips. "You rest. I'll do the talking." He eased his chair up close to the side of the bed.

"I acted like a jerk before, and I know it now," he admitted. "When I saw you hurt . . ." His face colored with embarrassment. "I remembered just how much you mean to me. I shouldn't have yelled at you about POE. It was wrong."

Nancy felt tears spring to her eyes. "Oh, Ned—" she began.

"But you don't know what I do about POE, Nan. I know they're in favor of good, sound environmental causes, but there's something wrong with that group. Don't ask me to prove it, because I can't. All I know is, Angela is a very impressionable and trusting girl. Too trusting—she's very easily led. A lot of POE's members are like that. You've got to believe me on this, Nan."

Nancy nodded, impressed by Ned's sincerity. He hesitated. "I know you're on some kind of secret mission here," he said. "And I know you're working hard on the case, whatever it is. But I'd like you to help me with this, too. Do you think you can?"

It only took Nancy a second to make up her mind. "If it's important to you, I'll help," she promised.

Ned leaned over for another hug.

"Ahem," someone cleared his throat behind them. Ned jumped back.

"How's the patient?" A good-looking man in a security uniform stepped into the room. He swept off his cap and settled into the other chair near Nancy's bed. "You look better now than you did lying facedown in the dirt, Ms. Drew."

Nancy eyed him curiously. "I take it you found me?"

"Ned and I found you," he replied, "out cold in the bushes."

"That's right," Ned added. "My conversation with Angela wasn't going anywhere, so I decided to catch up with you. You weren't at the dorm, so I guessed you might go to the science building since you said your investigation would begin there."

"On my security round I saw Ned, and we stumbled on you," the guard confirmed. "You were all alone. The guy who decked you was long gone."

"By the way, Nancy, this is Craig Bergin," Ned said as the guard stuck his hand out to Nancy. "Craig used to work at the gym, checking people's IDs."

Craig's hazel eyes twinkled. "And I got to know Ned really well—he always forgot his ID."

Nancy felt herself smiling at Craig's sunny personality. "Well, thanks for taking care of me." Nancy winced as a sharp pain shot through her head. She closed her eyes.

"Can you tell me what happened?" Craig asked. "Did somebody try to snatch your purse or something?"

Nancy looked questioningly at Ned, who nodded slightly. "Craig's a good guy," he told her.

Nancy smiled at Craig. "I don't think robbery was the motive."

"If you think of anything that might help me catch him, just let me know," Craig offered.

"I will," Nancy promised.

"I've got to go finish my report on you now. You can always find me at Campus Police headquarters."

"I've got to go, too, Nan," Ned said after Craig left. "My coach called a morning basketball practice."

"Basketball? But this is football season," Nancy said, surprised.

"We're playing one exhibition game this fall for charity. It's for a good cause, and I'll come back to see you before lunch."

"Whoa," Nancy objected. "I'm not hanging around the infirmary all day. There's someone out there who's pretty anxious to get rid of me. Besides, I've got work to do."

Ned frowned. "You can't go running around with that headache."

"There's nothing wrong with me that a few more aspirin won't cure. What do you want me to do? Sit here?"

Ned sighed and shook his head. "Why do I even try to argue? Look, let's compromise. Come with me to practice. That way I'll be able to keep an eye on you and make sure you're okay."

"Just sit there?" Nancy said doubtfully.

Ned grinned. "Well, you might chat with someone who knows a lot about Josef Maszak."

"Ned!" Nancy pretended to throw her pillow at him. "You're teasing. Who knows Professor Maszak?"

"Well, it's just a thought," Ned cautioned, "but I have seen Maszak with Coach Burnett. It's worth a try."

After collecting her things, Nancy followed Ned to the Emerson gym. There, Ned left

Nancy in the office with Coach Burnett, a tall, silver-haired man in his late fifties. Nancy was seated across from him in a red armchair, the only comfortable chair in the room. The coach leaned back and swung his feet onto his desk.

"I should have known you were here to investigate a mystery. Why don't you ever come up just to see us?" He broke into a smile that reached up to his gray eyes. "Or is Nickerson not as much of a hunk as all the cheerleaders think he is?"

Nancy blushed hotly. "Coach!"

The man laughed. "I'm sorry, Nancy, I shouldn't tease you. After all, I owe you a lot."

"Do you think we could get back to Professor Maszak?" Nancy asked.

"Sure. But I'm not sure how much I can tell you about him."

Nancy tried to hide her disappointment. "Ned said he'd seen you together."

"Well, we've had dinner a few times," Coach Burnett admitted. "But we don't talk about school or chemistry. I know very little personal background."

"At this point, anything would help," Nancy assured him.

Coach Burnett nodded thoughtfully. "Well, he's from Hungary, if you hadn't already guessed. His wife, Linda, is American, though, a linguist, I think. They met when she was teaching in Hungary. Stop me if this isn't the kind of thing you want."

"No, this is great," Nancy assured him.

The coach nodded. "Well, Linda's very sick. I'm not sure what's wrong, but I guess they decided she could get better medical treatment here. That's why they came to the States."

"That explains a lot," Nancy said. "I thought it was strange that a scientist from a communist country could come over here and do research for our government."

"Well, apparently it *was* a problem. Right now Maszak has only a working visa. He's waiting for permanent residency."

"Does he like it here?"

"Oh, yes," Coach Burnett said. "His first love is teaching. He loves his classes and his students love him."

"But he doesn't seem like a happy person," Nancy commented.

"Well, he's got a lot on his mind, with Linda and all. And I guess his work takes a lot out of him." The coach made a face. "All that fooling with biological mutations."

Nancy laughed. "Different people have different interests, I guess." She got up. "Thanks for everything, Coach."

"My pleasure, Nancy."

Nancy told Coach Burnett to tell Ned that he could find her in the science library. She headed straight there.

In the biology section she ran her fingers lightly over the bindings, working her way to the end of the aisle. Choosing a few books, she plopped down on the floor in the aisle and began paging through them. She didn't really know what she was looking for. Most of the information on biological mutations showed pictures of just that, mutations.

According to the books, Nancy found there were a few things you could do to an animal to make it grow larger and faster than usual. But the most common way to induce rapid growth was to give the animal a growth hormone. Nancy thought she remembered Maszak bragging about how young the huge carp actually was.

The books all said that the same hormone wouldn't affect different animals the same way, but Nancy was pretty sure that Maszak was using CLT on both the mice and the fish.

Maybe that was the big secret? CLT worked the same on all animals. Nancy frowned. She was no scientist, and her answers seemed all too easy. Nothing there for Dean Jarvis to get excited about. And nothing to involve the government.

Switching her attention to recent scientific

magazines, Nancy spent another hour poring through articles, many of which she didn't completely understand. Just as she was about to give up, she spotted an article describing the futile attempts to give different animals the same growth hormone. It was impossible that any growth hormone would work the same on all of them, the article said. Yet that seemed to be exactly what she had seen in Maszak's lab. Nancy's pulse quickened.

No one thought it could be done, yet she had seen it. A chill went up her spine. Forcing herself to remain calm, Nancy reread the article carefully. No doubt about it. There was only one growth hormone that could possibly achieve this result, the article said, and no one had access to that. It was very rare and unusual. And it could only come from a human!

Chapter Six

NANCY! I'VE BEEN LOOKING all over this place for you."

Startled, Nancy dropped her magazine. She looked up to see Ned towering over her.

Nancy gasped. "Ned," she cried, "you look terrible. Something's happened. What is it? What's wrong?"

Ned's face was grim. "It's Angela," he said. "She's gone."

"What are you talking about?" Nancy leapt to her feet, magazines slipping to the floor. "What do you mean she's gone?"

"Angela came to the frat house late last night

and talked to Mike. He said she was pretty upset. When he asked what was going on, she gave him a message for me. She said, 'Tell Ned I'm doing the right thing. Don't worry.' And today, when I went back there, this note was waiting for me."

Ned held up a piece of typing paper. "She says her belief in POE is destroying our friendship and she can't argue with me about it anymore. So she's left school. She's going to give all her time to them."

"Let me see that." Nancy took the paper from Ned and read it quickly. There was something about it—

"Wait a second, Ned, does Angela always type her letters?"

"As a matter of fact, she's taking a typing course right now. She's been typing everything all semester."

"Still"—Nancy shook her head—"she sounds very emotional. I wouldn't sit down and type a letter like this, would you?" She handed the letter back to Ned. "Why don't we pay this group a little visit?"

Ned grinned slyly. "I thought you'd never ask."

Ned helped Nancy shove the books and magazines back on the shelf. Then they made their way across campus as fast as possible.

The headquarters for POE were across a road

from the Emerson campus, in an abandoned business complex. Ned and Nancy followed a driveway that wound through the wooded grounds and ended in front of a large double-story building. Five smaller buildings were scattered among the trees along the road.

The gravelly driveway crunched under Nancy's feet as they approached the main building. No one came out to greet them. In fact, the place seemed deserted.

Ned glanced at Nancy. "Weird, huh?" he asked in a low voice.

Nancy nodded, slipping her hand securely into his. "You said they went on survival camp-outs on weekends. Maybe they left early."

The door to the main building was half open. It swung in noiselessly when Nancy pushed it. They stepped in.

Nancy and Ned found themselves in one large room, in what looked like a warehouse. There was a small, makeshift podium off to one side, with a stack of straw mats piled near it on the bare concrete floor. A delicate iron stairway was built in against the opposite wall, seeming to lead underground. The air inside was cold and smelled of forest dampness.

Twenty feet up on the walls, a catwalk circled the inside of the warehouse. A spiral staircase dropped to the main floor. Beyond the catwalk at one end, Nancy could see small rooms leading off from it. The center of the main room was open to the roof. As Nancy and Ned surveyed the area, a small figure appeared on the catwalk.

"Can I help you with something?" Nancy recognized Karen Lewis, the girl she had met in the arboretum.

"We came to see Angela Morrow." Ned's voice sounded hollow in the large space. "Can you tell us where to find her?"

As Karen headed down the spiral stairs, Nancy thought she saw a shadow lengthen along the wall of the room the girl had emerged from, but no one came out. As she approached, Karen looked at Nancy quizzically.

"Don't I know you?" she asked Nancy. "You look very familiar."

"I ran into your 'rehearsal' in the woods yesterday," Nancy reminded her.

"Oh, right." Karen flushed. "Nancy Drew. And now you're here about Angela?"

Nancy nodded, but Karen kept staring at her, as if she were waiting for her to talk about something else.

Ned shifted impatiently. "Yes," he prompted, "Angela Morrow. Can we see her?"

Karen turned her attention to him. "Right. Angela," she said, repeating his question. "She's not here, I'm afraid. I can leave a note for her if you'd like."

Nancy couldn't help thinking that Karen seemed distracted and a bit confused.

Ned locked eyes with Karen. "Angela left me a note saying she was coming to live here."

His words seemed to pull Karen out of her thoughts. She folded her arms across her chest. "As a matter of fact, she will be joining us here. But when students move off campus, they need parental consent. Angela went home to discuss it with her mom and dad."

Before Ned could reply, Nancy laid a hand on his arm to silence him.

"When people come here, where exactly do they stay?" she cut in, smoothly changing the subject. "I don't see any signs of people living here."

"This is just our meeting hall. There are a few offices up there on the catwalk, but no one lives here. We house people in the surrounding buildings. Right now, we have thirty full-time members," Karen boasted. "And we're still growing."

"Karen?" a deep voice boomed from the mezzanine.

They all turned toward the man who appeared on the catwalk.

"That's Philip Bangs," Nancy told Ned in a low voice. "The environmentalist. Angela talked about him the other night, remember?"

Philip Bangs swaggered down the stairs toward them. "Thanks, Karen, for letting me use your phone," he said. "I finally got ahold of the people at Saint Marks University and my speech *is* on for tomorrow. I appreciate your letting me stay but I have to leave for California now." Bangs turned to Nancy.

"It's Nancy Drew, right?" he said. Nancy was again struck by the force of his personality. She nodded.

"And I'm Ned Nickerson," Ned said, maneuvering himself between Bangs and Nancy. "Nice to meet you. We're looking for one of your members. Angela Morrow. Maybe you know her?"

Bangs laughed. "*My* members? I'd love to take the credit, but this is Karen's group. She founded POE. Actually, I've never seen or heard of another group like it. I'm just here because my lecture ran over yesterday and I missed my plane. She's got a great group of kids here," he said generously, clapping Karen on the shoulder warmly. "Earnest, committed—a wonderful group!"

Nancy watched Bangs curiously. For all his smooth manner, he didn't strike her as sincere.

Karen blushed at Bangs's compliment. "Philip, you remember Angela. The thin girl with the short black hair? You saw her off today when she went home."

Bangs furrowed his brow slowly. "Oh, yes!

Great kid. Very knowledgeable about politics, too."

"You saw her off?" Nancy interrupted. "You don't remember if she said anything, well, unusual, do you? Or if she left a message for anyone?"

"No, nothing unusual," Bangs replied. "She just jumped into her car and said she'd be back tomorrow."

Karen squared her shoulders and turned to Bangs. "Philip, before you go, I want to schedule another lecture sometime in the spring." The blond girl turned back to Nancy and Ned, dismissing them. "I'm sorry Angela isn't here, but we do expect her back tomorrow. I'll tell her you came by."

Nancy could see that Ned was about ready to burst. She led him outside quickly.

"Angela's father died when she was six years old!" Ned said furiously. "How could she be getting his permission? I don't believe a word they say. What if they're holding her against her will?"

Nancy hesitated. "Angela seemed ready to join them last night. Besides, what would they have to gain by holding her? Does her mother have a lot of money?"

Ned shook his head. "Not that I know of."

"Look, Ned, I hate to say it," Nancy pointed out quietly, "but it might mean nothing. Why would Karen know if Angela's father was alive or not?"

"It doesn't fit," Ned insisted.

Nancy nodded. "You're right. I don't like this, either, but we won't know more until we talk to Angela."

"I could call her at home."

Nancy took Ned's arm. "Ned, you talked your heart out last night and it didn't work. I don't think you'll change her mind now. Let's wait and see what happens when she gets back."

Nancy walked Ned to his history class. He still seemed moody and distracted. Stopping to let the boisterous crowd of students pass them, she gave him a quick kiss and made him promise not to worry. As Nancy watched Ned disappear into the gray stone building, she couldn't help thinking something *was* wrong with POE. She ached to help him find out what it was, but she was here at Emerson to solve a different mystery and she'd better get started.

Heading for the science building, Nancy spied Professor Maszak shouting into a pay phone. Seeing her, he lowered his voice and turned his back on her.

Nancy drifted into one of the phone booths a few feet away, lifted the receiver and pretended to dial. She strained to hear what Maszak was saying but his words were too soft. Then, just as she prepared to give up, he raised his voice.

"I'm doing it," she heard him growl. "I've been doing it all along, and they haven't done anything with it! *They* are the ones wasting time waiting for the processing. You'll get your money. I'll go back to them and see what I can do. You can count on me."

There was a short silence, then Maszak exploded again. "Don't tell me this is important. It's more important to me than it is to you. To me, this is a matter of life or death!"

Chapter Seven

BEFORE NANCY COULD REACT, Professor Maszak slammed down the receiver and stalked away. She filed the conversation away. What was a matter of life or death? If Maszak was hiding important information from her, she wanted to know what and why.

Nancy placed the receiver in its cradle slowly. As a good detective, she knew never to rule out any suspect, no matter how innocent he or she might seem. In fact, it was often the people who seemed most innocent who were most guilty. Maszak could be involved in the thefts himself.

As Nancy hurried after the rumpled professor, she thought about the explosion in the lab. When the beaker blew up, Maszak had been surprisingly understanding about Sara's clumsy mistake. Was he *too* understanding?

Tossing her head back with determination, Nancy resolved to find out as much as she could. If Maszak was lying, he was very good at it. Nancy decided she'd have better luck with Sara.

Turning, Nancy picked up the telephone again and called student information. In no time she'd found Sara's dorm and her room number.

Slipping through the busy lobby, Nancy quietly made her way down the long dorm hallway. Without pausing, she knocked on Sara's door. There was no answer. "Bad luck," Nancy murmured to herself. Now she'd have to waste time tracking Sara down. She knocked once more to make sure, and to her surprise the door pushed open.

Nancy hesitated. Sara wasn't a suspect in the thefts, but she could be. And she might learn something from a quick search of Sara's room.

Inside, the late-afternoon sun bounced off the large mirror over the dresser on one wall. Opposite it, a standard-issue Formica desk was surrounded by posters of animals in the wild. Sara's bed was neatly made.

Moving swiftly, Nancy checked the desk drawers. Finding nothing unusual, she flipped through the looseleaf binders lying in neat stacks on the desk. Sara's notes were written in small, careful script. There was no chemistry notebook, Nancy noted. Sara might have that one with her. None of the other notebooks mentioned Maszak's experiments or CLT.

The bright sunshine playing off the dresser caught Nancy's attention. Among bottles of perfume and makeup samples was a familiar object. Nancy picked it up. A bronze-colored snake earring—the same as the ones worn by Karen Lewis and Angela Morrow.

Nancy felt suddenly chilled. Sara was a POE member, too. That was one coincidence she hadn't expected. Was the group somehow connected to Professor Maszak's research? Even to the theft of the CLT? Had they learned of Maszak's animal experiments? And were they trying to stop them?

Nancy stepped up her search, pulling open drawers, looking for anything that might link the CLT thefts to the environmental group. She heard a noise at the door and saw the doorknob turning. She barely had time to shove the drawer shut and whirl around before the door opened. Sara Hughes's chunky body was framed in the doorway.

Sara stared at Nancy in confusion. "What are you doing here?" she demanded.

"Looking for you," Nancy answered. Her voice sounded surprisingly calm. "I have some questions I'd like to ask you."

"About that story you're writing, right?" Sara eyed Nancy suspiciously. "Shouldn't you have called first?"

Nancy pretended to be a hard-nosed reporter without manners. "Your door was open," she said, shrugging. "I decided to wait here."

"Oh. Well, I guess that's okay." Sara waved her hand at the desk chair and Nancy sat down.

"This is a very important story, Sara," Nancy said. "I need to know exactly what you do for Professor Maszak. For instance," she said casually, "what were you doing last night in the chemistry lab?"

Sara's face went white. Then, without warning, she burst into tears.

"I didn't do anything wrong," she wailed. "I was only trying to catch up on all my work. I've fallen so far behind, and—I don't know what to do!"

Surprised at this outburst, Nancy shifted awkwardly in her seat waiting for Sara's sobbing to subside. "Sara," she asked gently, "do you want to tell me about it?"

Sara took a deep breath. "I'm just so scared,"

she confessed, her voice trembling. "My father lost his job this summer and hasn't been able to find a new one. He's been doing part-time work, but I don't know whether he'll be able to send me back to school next semester."

"What does that have to do with the lab?" Nancy asked.

"Everything!" Sara cried. "I've applied for every scholarship there is, but so far I haven't heard. I'm so upset I can't concentrate on anything. The more I worry, the more I seem to mess up. Professor Maszak already warned me —if I don't shape up, I'll lose my job in the lab."

The anguish on Sara's face was genuine. Her eyes brimmed with tears. "I've been so nervous," she went on. "Between the mistakes I'm making and the thef— I mean, well, I may not have my job for long."

"Thefts," Nancy repeated. "You were going to say thefts."

Sara looked at Nancy with alarm. "No one knows about the thefts—only me and the professor." She drew away suddenly. "Who are you, anyway? I don't believe you're a student reporter at all."

Nancy took a deep breath. "I'll be straight with you, Sara, since you've already guessed the truth. You have to promise me, though, that this is strictly between you and me. If not, the professor could be hurt. Emerson could be hurt."

Sara paled. "I swear, I won't tell anyone. I'd never do that."

Nancy believed her. She had a strong feeling that Sara was no thief. "I'm here to investigate the thefts of the CLT. I'm helping Dean Jarvis."

"Are you from the government?" Sara's eyes widened.

"No way," Nancy assured her. "I'm a private detective. I care about Emerson College, and I don't want to see the school suffer because of the thefts."

Sara reddened and went to her desk, drawing a tissue from a drawer. "So that's what you were really doing in my room. You thought I stole the CLT."

"I don't now," Nancy said honestly. "Sara—will you help me?"

"I doubt if I can." Sara's voice was flat. "All I know is, the CLT was stolen each time right before we were about to begin the experiment."

"Is there something particularly important about that time?"

"No," Sara said helplessly. "It's just another stage in the process. The professor gets the stuff, he treats it, and then we start the experiment."

"Do you help with the treatment?" Nancy asked.

"No one does," Sara said. "He's very secretive about the whole process. I just try to stay out of his way."

Nancy nodded. "Who else knows when Maszak has finished the treatment?"

"The professor, me, and Dean Jarvis."

"No one else? No students?"

"No. But the professor keeps a daily log of the experiment on his computer. I've never seen his entries."

Nancy felt a faint twinge of excitement. "But someone could get into the program and find out that way," she suggested.

Sara frowned. "I doubt it. There's a secret password. No one but the professor knows what it is."

"It doesn't sound good for the professor," Nancy muttered.

"I know," Sara cried. "Ever since the CLT was first taken, I've tried to figure out who did it." She paused and looked at Nancy pleadingly. "But I know one thing—there's no reason for Professor Maszak to take it."

"You're probably right," Nancy admitted. "Maszak has the most to lose if this gets out. And if he needed the CLT for unauthorized experiments, he could have found a better way to get it."

Unless, she thought to herself, he got too greedy. Nancy remembered the telephone conversation she had overheard. CLT was rare and valuable—Maszak said so himself. He also had a sick wife whose treatment was very expensive. Nancy didn't want to alarm Sara, but Maszak had a very good reason to steal the CLT: so he could sell it and pocket the money.

With Sara eliminated, Maszak became Nancy's number-one suspect. But that didn't explain the connection to POE.

Casually, Nancy rose and picked up the earring from Sara's dresser.

"This is a great earring," she said, holding the bronze snake to her ear and modeling it in the mirror. "I've never seen one quite like it."

Sara sighed distractedly. "Oh, that's not mine. I found it in the lab this morning. It must belong to a POE member. I asked around in morning and afternoon science classes and I even put a note on the bulletin board, but no one's claimed it yet, so I brought it back here."

"Oh?" Nancy was intrigued. She turned to look at Sara. "Are there many POE members in your classes?"

"Oh, yes! Well, I mean, there are a couple hundred students in the lab each day. Freshman biology, advanced chemistry courses, there are tons of students in and out. Emerson requires everyone to complete two semesters of a lab science to graduate. The classes are extra popular this year because of Professor Maszak's reputation."

Nancy dangled the earring between her fingers. "Do you mind if I keep this until it's claimed?"

"No. I'll call you if I need it back. Maybe tomorrow—" Sara stopped suddenly.

"Is something wrong?" Nancy asked, concerned.

"Tomorrow." Sara turned her face toward Nancy's. "The professor got his new CLT two days ago. He'll be finished treating it tomorrow. That means—"

"If the thief is going to strike again, it will happen tomorrow," Nancy finished for her. She placed a hand on Sara's shoulder. "Don't worry. This time, we'll stop the person, whoever it is."

As Nancy headed back to her dorm, she wished she was as sure of herself as she had tried to make Sara believe. She had only one day to stop the thief. She was going to have to come up with some answers, and fast.

After a quick dinner, Nancy returned to her room where she collapsed in a chair. It was late, and her head was beginning to ache where she'd been hit. She decided to take a shower and go to bed. Ned had a late practice, so they wouldn't be seeing each other until the next day.

As she went to the closet to grab her robe, Nancy noticed the doorknob on the closet door was smeared with a brownish film. She hadn't seen it that morning when she left.

Uneasily, she wondered what it could be. She checked the rest of the room quickly, but nothing had been disturbed. It was probably nothing, but then again, she wasn't about to take any chances.

Looking around, Nancy spotted a pencil on her bedside table. She picked it up. Going back to the closet, she paused. Gingerly, holding the pencil away from her body, she bent the tip to scrape off a dab of the film. That way, she could examine it.

Nancy gingerly touched the pencil point to the doorknob. But the instant the tip touched the brown film, there was a huge flash. Then, with a thunderous boom, the door exploded off its hinges and came crashing—right at Nancy.

Chapter Eight

"WHO WOULD HAVE DONE such a thing? Do you have any enemies at Emerson?" Paul Osborne, the chief security guard, bent over a pad as he made notes on the condition of the ruined closet door. His scalp was shiny with perspiration.

Nancy perched on the end of her bed as Osborne and another security guard checked the damage. The dorm counselor who had sounded the alarm hovered anxiously in the doorway.

"I don't have any enemies here," Nancy replied innocently, with one eye on the counselor.

Osborne lowered himself into a chair, leaving the second guard to finish the job.

"You're lucky you didn't touch the knob with your hands," he said. "That glop doesn't look like much, but it sure packs a wallop."

"Exactly what is it?" Nancy asked. "And where would someone at Emerson get it?"

"Anyone can get it," Osborne said grimly. "You could buy the ingredients at any pharmacy. Two common, safe household items, but put them together and paint it on something and once it's dry—well, you saw the results."

Nancy looked at the ruined closet and shuddered. The door was charred and burned, hanging limply on its hinges. The blow had knocked her to her feet, and she had gotten a bad fright from the shock of the explosion. The fingers on her right hand were burned slightly, but other than that, she was unhurt.

"Then this explosive could be made by anyone who knows a little chemistry," she mused. "But how did you know what it was? Have you seen it before?"

Osborne patted his forehead with a handkerchief. "Actually," he said slowly, "we've seen it three other times. Always on doorknobs. The other times, no one got hurt because they blew when no one was around. It's probably some nut who likes to make explosions. Too bad you didn't come back earlier—you might have caught him in the act. I'd sure like to know who it is."

"We'll have to ask you to check the room to make sure nothing is missing, Ms. Drew," the younger guard called from inside the closet. His round face appeared around the ruined door frame. "Was there anything valuable in your closet?"

"No," Nancy said. "The door to my room wasn't even locked."

"Uh-huh," Osborne nodded knowingly. "Nothing was taken the other times, either. See what I mean? Must have been done by a crank, someone who discovered the mixture and thinks it's a big joke. You're sure you don't have any enemies here?"

Nancy hesitated but then shook her head. If Dean Jarvis had wanted campus security to know, he would have told them about the thefts in the chemistry lab.

Osborne got ready to go. "Well, I'm just glad you weren't hurt. We'll keep investigating, and I may call you later to ask you more questions. If you think of anything that could help us, just give me a call."

"You should call the police," the counselor said angrily.

"Oh, no, wouldn't want to do that," Osborne

warned. "The college likes to keep this kind of thing as quiet as possible." He straightened his shoulders. "Besides, we can handle our own 'police work.' "

"Wait, please," Nancy said. "Can you tell me which other doors were tampered with?"

Osborne looked at her with surprise. "Does it matter? Well, if you must know, the first was the main door to the library. The librarian got there and found a big hole where the knob had been. Then the computer room blew."

"No, the library wasn't first," the other guard contradicted. "The cafeteria was."

"Oh, that's right." Osborne chuckled. "The main cafeteria door was blown wide open. Now, why would anyone want to break in and steal *that* food?" He laughed heartily at his own joke.

"Was anything stolen?" Nancy persisted. Osborne shook his head. "That seems very strange. Why blow up a door if you don't want to get inside? The three must have something in common—the same area, maybe?"

"You certainly ask a lot of questions." Osborne frowned. "But, no, they're spread out all over campus. I wouldn't worry about those other explosions. The more I think about it, the more I've decided yours isn't related. They were set to damage buildings. This one seems to have been set against you."

Nancy sighed in frustration. If there was a connection, she couldn't see it. If she *was* close to catching the thief, she didn't even know it. Well, she was going to get even closer, Nancy resolved, explosion or no explosion!

Nancy spent the next morning investigating everyone who had anything to do with the lab. She spoke to the security guards who were on duty the nights of the thefts. Both men swore they were alert and awake the whole time, and that they had seen no one.

Nancy tried to get through to Dean Jarvis during the day, but he was in meetings until four. She called again at four, only to be told that the dean was on a long-distance call and couldn't be disturbed. She tried to keep her frustration under control.

"This is Nancy Drew speaking. I've been trying to reach Dean Jarvis since this morning. It's very important. I'd really appreciate it if I could hold while you let him know I'm on the line."

Nancy waited. A minute or so later someone else picked up the phone, and Nancy found herself explaining her situation all over again, only to be put back on hold. In the next few minutes she spoke with five different secretaries and told each of them it was an emergency.

Well, Nancy thought, forgiving herself for her white lie, if she didn't get ahold of the dean soon, it could very well become an emergency.

Just as she was losing her patience altogether, Nancy heard a couple of clicks as if the dean had picked up, and then another.

"Nancy?" It was the dean's voice. Quickly, she filled him in on her suspicions.

"Are you *sure* the thief will strike again tonight?" the dean asked worriedly. "I could assign all my guards to the building, but you'd have to be sure."

"No, if he sees any of them we'll never catch him," Nancy objected. "With Ned and me and a couple of security guards on duty, I don't think he can get away."

"I don't know, Nancy. I'm responsible for your safety. I'd feel a lot better if you had some backup."

Nancy promised to be careful. "We don't need help. Ned will be out near the elevators with the guard. If you assign one extra man to watch the outer doors, we ought to have plenty of warning when an intruder enters. I'll hide in Maszak's lab. That should make the lab pretty burglarproof."

"Wait," the dean said, "you'll need to know the combination to get into the interior lab. Did you get it from Josef?"

"Actually, I haven't said anything to Professor Maszak about tonight," Nancy said carefully. "It has to be absolutely secret. The fewer people who know about it, the better."

Nancy heard a click on the line. "Dean Jarvis?" she asked. "Are you still there?"

"Yes, why?"

"I thought I heard you hang up the telephone."

"That happens all the time—these huge telephone networks. Don't worry about it. About tonight, though, I'll alert the campus police to keep their eyes open and their radios on. In fact, I want you and Ned to stop by their headquarters and pick up two walkie-talkies so you can call for help."

After giving Nancy the combination to the lock, the dean hung up.

At dusk Nancy and Ned met at the lab. Ned had agreed to go along with her plan even though Nancy couldn't explain all the details. She had promised Dean Jarvis, after all, and somehow didn't feel right about letting Ned in on what was top secret work. Luckily he understood. Meanwhile, Dean Jarvis had arranged for Craig Bergin to be the guard on duty.

"Someone got me reassigned," he told them happily. "Just in time. It's a little too cold to have to patrol the campus at night. I've been asked to keep my eye on the lab."

Nancy and Ned exchanged quick looks.

"Great!" Nancy said. "I'll be working in the lab all night tonight. Um, it's a special arrangement, for that story I'm writing."

"Yes, and I'll be just outside with this, just to make sure things go smoothly," Ned said, patting the walkie-talkie.

Craig shrugged. "Suits me. I'll be glad to have someone to talk to."

Nancy worked the combination to Maszak's office effortlessly. After checking with Ned on the walkie-talkie, she promised to check back in an hour. She set the walkie-talkie down on the long counter and perched on Maszak's stool. There were papers strewn all over the top as well as two big stacks of notebooks. A quick glance told Nancy they were Maszak's students' experiments.

Nancy shuffled through the notebooks. The experiments seemed fairly standard. She checked idly through the advanced biology and chemistry classes, keeping an eye out for any names she might recognize. There were none.

Sighing, she picked up another pile of papers —Maszak's advanced biochemistry students, proposing their final projects. She went through them, noting names and grades and reading Maszak's comments. The experiments were incredible! Some of them were straight out of sci-fi films. One paper in particular caught

Nancy's attention. Maszak had slashed a purple felt-tip pen across the first page and scrawled notes in the top margin.

Looking more closely, Nancy's heart began to pound. The subject of the paper was human growth hormones.

Chapter Nine

WITH A GROWING SENSE of excitement, Nancy read on. The paper suggested some of the same things she had read in the startling article in the library. The student planned an experiment to see if one kind of animal could accept a growth hormone from another kind of animal. Then, at the very end of the paper, she suggested someday trying a human growth hormone. Maszak's comments were angry and critical, impatiently explaining why the experiment was doomed to fail. He gave the student an incomplete and suggested she pick another topic.

Nancy frowned. If her hunch was correct, the

student wasn't wrong at all—she had simply come dangerously close to copying Maszak's own experiment. With an eerie feeling, Nancy stared at the fish and mice in the lab. Had Maszak already made a major breakthrough? Had he been using a human growth hormone on animals? Was CLT a human growth hormone?

The floorboards in the hall creaked loudly. Quickly Nancy scattered the papers across the counter again. She ducked into a closet and held her breath.

The lab door opened. She could hear someone moving around. At the same instant, she realized her walkie-talkie wasn't with her. She had left it on Maszak's counter. What an amateurish thing to do! She could kick herself.

Concentrating, Nancy pictured the counter in her mind, trying to remember where she had left the walkie-talkie before taking refuge in the closet. Hopefully, it was buried under the stacks of papers. If it wasn't hidden, the thief might realize someone was there. Even worse, Nancy realized as her stomach took a sickening plunge, there was no way now for her to contact Ned.

Pressing the light on her watch, Nancy saw it was nine o'clock. An hour had passed since she last checked in. Ned might come down to see if she was all right. Together, the two of them might be able to overpower the thief—if it *was* the thief out there.

Whoever it was, he was taking his time in the lab. Nancy heard footsteps pacing. Then there was a grunt and something fell to the floor near the closet door. Nancy froze. Pressing her ear against the door, she could hear faint scratching sounds. The seconds passed like minutes. Finally she heard the lab door open and close. Fine, she told herself. I'll just let another minute pass to make sure it's safe to come out.

But before the minute went by, a faint smell of smoke wafted through the bottom of the closet. Nancy put her hand against the closet door. It was warm to the touch. The closet door was on fire!

Nancy yelled for Ned as she snatched some lab coats off the hangers around her. Wrapping one of them around her head to protect her face from the smoke, she grabbed another pile of coats to smother the flames. Taking a deep breath, she leaned against the door. It resisted her efforts. The smoke was getting thicker now. Choking, she leaned against the door, even harder. It gave way and she stumbled into the source of the smoke.

Outside the door, the student notebooks had been piled high and set on fire. The flames licked at Nancy's ankles. She was dimly aware of a smoke alarm sending its piercing warning through the halls as she threw the lab coats down in front of her, trying to smother the burning barricade. She leapt over the notebooks, landing on the floor with a thud. Groaning, she rolled away from the fire.

Half crawling, she made her way to the freezer unit against the far wall. With her last ounce of strength, she pried the door open. The CLT was gone.

"Nan, Nan, where are you?"

Ned and Craig burst into the room. Craig grabbed the fire extinguisher on the wall and began spraying the fire as Ned rushed to help Nancy.

"I-I'm fine." Coughing and choking from the smoke, Nancy clung gratefully to Ned. He swept her into his arms and stumbled into the hallway.

"We'll get you to the infirmary, Nan. Just hang on." Ned's voice was choked, from the smoke or his own emotion, she couldn't tell. "You're going to be okay."

Nancy sat up in bed late the next afternoon. "The infirmary nurse says I'm just fine now," she assured Ned. "Look, I didn't even get burned, and I've slept all day."

She held up her hands, and Ned grabbed them in his and kissed them.

"The invincible Nancy Drew." He grinned.

"Goes through fire without blinking an eye. I'm beginning to wonder why I ever worry about you." Ned sank into the chair next to her bed and closed his eyes wearily.

Nancy's eyes clouded with sympathy. "I'm sorry, Ned," she said softly, "I didn't mean to drag you into this case."

Ned leaned close, grinning ruefully. "I guess it proves I'd go through raging fires for you."

How did she get such a wonderful guy? Nancy thought as she burrowed her head into Ned's shoulder. "I don't know what I would have done," she admitted. Her throat closed as she realized how close she'd come to real danger. "If you hadn't been there . . ."

"Shhh," Ned whispered. "What I don't understand is how the thief got past both me and Craig in the hall. It doesn't seem possible."

"It can happen. Don't blame yourself—please. The thief was determined," Nancy said.

Drawing Nancy close, Ned rocked her gently, landing a soft kiss on her hair. "You smell like smoke," he said, laughing.

"Ned, I'm sorry I couldn't tell you what this was about," Nancy began.

"I understand," he told her.

Nancy decided then it was time to take Ned into her confidence. Clearly, she hadn't learned the thief's identity in time to stop the next CLT theft. She was willing to admit she needed help. Quickly, she explained everything to Ned.

"Excuse me, I was told you could have visitors." Nancy and Ned looked up as Dean Jarvis stuck his head into the room. "Am I interrupting something?"

"Dean Jarvis, is there anything new?" Nancy saw him glance at Ned. "It's okay. I told Ned everything. I had to."

The dean hesitated, then nodded abruptly. "Good. Well, then, I checked with security," the dean reported. "As soon as Ned sounded the alarm, they shut all the gates and set up checkpoints at all the campus entrances. As far as we know, no one left campus with the CLT. It's in a pretty big container, after all. There's a good chance it's still on campus."

"I hope so," Nancy said fervently. "I'd hate to think that I sat in the closet while the thief got away."

"It couldn't be helped, Nancy," the dean assured her.

Nancy shrugged. "Did anyone figure out how the thief got in?"

Dean Jarvis shook his head. "No. But don't worry about it. It's not your problem anymore. I'm taking you off the case."

"What?" Nancy gasped.

"It's too dangerous," the dean said firmly.

"This person means business. I can't take the chance that you'll get hurt."

"But, Dean Jarvis, I'm really close now," Nancy objected. "I didn't really get hurt. I'm okay now. Please—I know I can wrap up the case. I just need a little more time."

The dean was unmoved. He didn't say a word, only shook his head again.

"Please, sir? It would save you a lot of trouble. And besides," Nancy added recklessly, "how will it look if you call in the government now? They'll want to know why you didn't report the thefts immediately. If I solve the case and recover the CLT, they can't say a thing."

"Well, when you put it like that . . ." Dean Jarvis began. He paused. "No, I still can't."

"I can solve this case for you," Nancy insisted. "I'm very close already."

"I don't know." The dean wavered.

Nancy smiled. "Think of Emerson. Your science program."

"All right!" The dean threw up his hands. "But only if you promise to come to me at the first sign of trouble."

Ned waited silently until Dean Jarvis had gone.

"Are you really that close, Nan?" he burst out as soon as the dean's footsteps had faded away.

"Almost." Eagerly, Nancy swung her legs off the bed. "And I will solve it soon. Right now, we'd better get over to the lab and find out how the thief got in."

"There's no use in my trying to stop you, is there?" Nancy shook her head. Sighing, Ned went out to wait in the hall while Nancy got dressed.

By the time Nancy and Ned got back to the lab, the mess from the fire had been cleaned up. She could tell from the fine white dust in the room that the campus police had checked for fingerprints.

The room still reeked of smoke. On the desk Nancy found the walkie-talkie hidden under some papers. The thief hadn't bothered to take it.

"Nothing new here," Nancy said. "Let's check with your friend Craig."

Nancy explained to Craig that Dean Jarvis had allowed them to follow up on what had happened. "The story's getting more involved than I thought," she added when he gave them a confused look.

Craig shrugged and looked as baffled as Nancy. "I checked with all the guards myself," he told her. "I even had someone watching the fire escape. The elevators, which weren't in service, were locked for the night. I have no idea how he got in."

"Well, you don't mind if we check around a bit, do you?" Ned asked.

"Not at all. Here." Craig threw his key ring to Ned. "These keys will open everything in the building. Yell if you find anything."

Out in the main hall, Nancy and Ned tried to decide where to go next. Ned leaned back against a closet door, thinking.

"It's a waste of time to check the rooms on this floor," he said. "Security's already checked them all."

Nancy's eyes lit up and a grin spread across her face. "Maybe not all," she said slowly. "Ned—take a step toward me."

"Huh?" Baffled, Ned approached, not sure if Nancy was joking or not.

"That's fine." Grinning, Nancy ducked behind him. "This closet," she said. "We've been looking so hard for big clues, we didn't try the little ones."

The closet was locked. Pulling out Craig's key ring, Nancy tried each key. None of them opened the door.

"Oh, don't worry about that door," Craig said, coming into the hall. "There's nothing behind it."

"You mean the closet is empty?" Nancy asked.

"It's not a closet," Craig said. "It's an old elevator shaft. There was a freight elevator there. You know the kind that works with a key? It hasn't been used in years."

Nancy's pulse quickened. "Is the elevator still there? Does it work?"

"I don't see how it could. They shut it down years ago because it was unsafe. No one in his right mind would get into the thing, even if he could."

Nancy was examining the door, inch by inch. "Ned, Craig—look at this," she suddenly called. "There."

Nancy pointed to a thin crack. It ran around the perimeter of the door. "Someone used this elevator recently," she insisted. "When the door opened, it cracked through these old layers of paint."

Ned and Craig exchanged a look. "You're right," Ned said. "Good work, Nan."

Nancy found a piece of wire and went to work on the lock. She twisted it until she felt something give. With a triumphant smile, she opened the door.

The elevator shaft fell off in front of her. Grabbing Ned's hand to anchor herself, she leaned in and peered down. "How do we call the elevator?"

Craig gestured to another lock on the wall just outside the door. "I guess you can pick this lock. You used to need a key to call the elevator."

Nancy set about trying to open the old lock. Finally it clicked, and she heard the old elevator car creaking up the shaft.

"Sounds like it's been used recently," she murmured. "The thief must have put it in working order."

As they watched, a black cage rose out of the gloom and glided to a halt. Nancy grabbed the handle and pulled the iron accordion door to one side. "Anyone coming with me?" she invited.

Craig and Ned looked at each other uneasily. "It's pretty old—do you think it will carry three of us?" Craig asked.

Nancy's eyes twinkled. "There's only one way to find out."

Chapter Ten

NANCY TRIED the old elevator lever. It moved easily. Hurriedly, Ned and Craig hopped on, too. She pushed the lever to the right and the cage began to rise. Through the grate, they could see the rough cement walls of the shaft. They passed the fourth- and fifth-floor doors. The elevator stopped on the top floor. The door to the roof level was locked.

"If our thief went to the roof, he'd have to climb down without being seen," Nancy said. "Not very likely. Let's see what happens when we go down."

She threw the switch to the left. Seven

floors went by. The elevator settled at the bottom.

"This must be the lobby," Craig commented as he reached for the door.

Nancy shook her head. "No, the building only has six floors. I counted seven. This has to be the basement."

Craig looked at her in surprise. "There *is* no basement," he said.

Ignoring Craig for the moment, Nancy pushed against the outside door. It swung open noiselessly. Stepping out, they found themselves in a small, damp gray room. A light next to the elevator door cast dark shadows around them.

Craig whistled softly. "Well, I'll be—" he exclaimed.

"I'll bet this is the thief's escape route," Nancy whispered excitedly.

The space was empty except for a cobweb-covered fuse box on one wall. A black hole in the wall directly opposite the elevator led to a passageway. There was another passageway on their right. At the end of each, Nancy saw a thin glow of light.

"These are tunnels!" Nancy said, amazed. "It looks like they connect the basements of the buildings."

"That's right," Craig said excitedly. "I've

heard the old maintenance guys talking about using the tunnels in the old days to get from building to building. I thought they'd all been sealed up."

"They're unsealed now," Nancy said grimly. She took a step toward one.

"Nan, hold on." Grasping her elbow, Ned pulled her back. "It's late and it's dark in there. Whoever stole the CLT left almost twenty-four hours ago. Wouldn't it be better to come back tomorrow—with a good flashlight?"

Ned was right, Nancy realized. "Okay," she said reluctantly. "Let's go back to the dorm and plan our next move."

They left Craig at the lab and headed over to Holland. Nancy and Ned had barely entered the lounge when Jan and Mike burst into the room with a girl Nancy had never met. She was wearing a bulky white sweater and green wool pants, and she had curly dark red hair that swung halfway down her back.

Breathlessly, Jan introduced them. "Nancy, this is Amber Thomas. She's Angela Morrow's roommate," Jan explained. "And she's got bad news."

Nancy and Ned exchanged startled glances.

"We'd better sit down," Nancy said.

"Nancy, this isn't like Angela at all," Amber cried. "She was supposed to come back today.

She didn't, so I called her house." Amber took a deep breath. "Her mom hadn't seen her. Angela never went home."

"That does it," Ned declared angrily. "I'm going to find her."

Nancy knew better than to try to talk Ned out of it. "At this point," she said slowly, "I think that's the best thing for you to do. But, Ned," she added, "you should wait until morning, too."

Ned smiled. "It's a deal. I'd better get to bed so I can get an early start. Good night, Nan. And don't you guys worry—I'll call as soon as I find out anything."

After a night of troubled sleep, Nancy was hurrying to the science building. As she passed the infirmary, a commotion in the doorway caught her attention. A girl with a shower of long blond hair was pleading with the nurse at the front door. It was Karen Lewis. A brown bundle lay at her feet. Looking closer, Nancy saw it was an injured dog. Curious, Nancy walked over to see what was going on.

Karen was very distraught. She had found the dog by the side of the road and was begging the nurse to take a look at it.

"But I'm not a veterinarian," the nurse kept repeating. "I treat *people.* I don't know the first thing about dogs."

"There must be something you can do," Karen insisted wildly. "If you don't, the poor thing's going to die."

Nancy was right behind them now. "Excuse me," she cut in. Karen whirled around at the sound of her voice. "Maybe there *is* something you could do," she suggested. "Could you describe the dog's condition to a vet? There must be one in Emersonville we could call."

"Well, I guess so," the nurse said uncertainly.

"I'll pay for the call," Karen burst out. The nurse nodded and went inside.

Karen stood silently next to Nancy, avoiding her eyes.

"Is it your dog?" Nancy asked lightly, trying not to put Karen off.

Karen shook her head. "I found it. I was hiking all morning, and when I returned I saw it beside the highway on the edge of the campus."

"And you carried it here?" Nancy was surprised.

"Does everyone think I'm crazy to help this dog?" Karen challenged. "If it was your dog, you'd be happy."

"Sorry," Nancy offered. "You did the right thing."

The nurse returned, smiling happily. "I reached a vet, and he said he was going out and would stop by here." She bent down and put her hands on the dog's side. "He said to check his gums to make sure they aren't too white or too red, take his pulse, and keep him warm."

As Karen bent to stroke the injured animal, Nancy backed away. Karen was certainly sincere in her love for animals. She was even softhearted about animals that didn't belong to her. Perhaps Nancy was wrong to distrust POE and its members. Ned might be confusing his concern for Angela with his feelings about the group.

There was too much going on, Nancy told herself with a sigh. First the CLT mystery, now the trouble with Angela and POE. At least she felt closer to solving *one* mystery now.

Nancy decided against tackling the tunnels under Emerson without more information. She went to the library and buried herself in a pile of books about the architecture of Emerson. After two books, she found what she was looking for—a series of drawings showing the extensive tunnel system. It spread to every one of the original buildings on campus. The map also confirmed that none of the tunnels went beyond the campus. The thief had to be holding the stolen CLT somewhere on the grounds, Nancy decided.

She was eager to begin her search of the tunnels, but an uneasy feeling nagged at her. She had to check a little further. On a hunch, she went to the section where microfilms of the local newspapers were kept. In the *Emersonian*, the school's paper, she found a feature article on Josef Maszak. It mentioned that he had come from Jamison College, another midwestern school, where he had taught for three years. The Jamison students had given him the Beller Award for excellence in teaching three years in a row.

Nancy remembered the loyalty both Sara and Angela had shown toward Maszak. He really did inspire his students, she realized. Jamison College was in the same sports league as Emerson, and the library kept a record of its rival's papers. Nancy searched that microfilm, too, stopping at the issues that came out when Maszak was at Jamison.

A headline caught her eye: BACTERIA DESTROYED IN LAB. She felt a tingle of excitement as she read.

> One of the school's most important experiments involving five different kinds of bacteria had to be destroyed yesterday in the science lab. A sample of rheumatic fever, a disease caused by bacteria, had begun growing out of control. Professor Aaron Miller, who was in charge of the project, was quoted as saying, "We have no idea what happened. The bacteria grew so quickly that we had to take extreme mea-

sures to destroy it. Unfortunately, by destroying the bacteria, we also destroyed the cause of its abnormal growth. Now we'll never know what brought this about." No damage or injuries were reported.

There was no mention of Josef Maszak, but he had been at Jamison at this time. Nancy flipped through the rest of the film. Toward the end of the reel, an ad caught her eye. It announced a lecture series on Third World countries. Dr. Pranav Mohammed would discuss famine relief that Tuesday, and consumer advocate Philip Bangs would lecture on the evils of chemical weapons. The lecture series was sponsored by POE.

Nancy froze. Environmentalist groups were probably common at schools, but she was sure Philip Bangs had said Karen Lewis had created POE at Emerson. He had even said there were no other POE groups! He had been lying.

With a start, Nancy remembered the earring Sara had found in the lab. No one had ever claimed it. Was it because its owner couldn't admit to having been in the lab?

This was more than a coincidence, Nancy thought with certainty. The same secret group, the same speaker, and the same professor—they had to be connected, but how?

Chapter Eleven

NANCY NEARLY FLEW across campus. She held her purse steady, glad she had taken the time to make a copy of the tunnel map.

On the map, she noticed the tunnels led to a dorm only fifty feet from Adams Cottage, where Professor Maszak lived. Nancy intended to take that route herself. If it was unblocked, Maszak would have both a motive and an opportunity for stealing the CLT himself. He'd have a lot of explaining to do, Nancy thought grimly. Philip Bangs might very well be part of his explanation.

After heading straight for the science building, Nancy picked the lock on the freight elevator and stepped inside. The elevator creaked down to the basement. Nancy slid the door open and stepped out cautiously, waiting for her eyes to adjust to the weak light. She pulled out her map and held it under the bare yellow bulb mounted on the cement wall.

According to the drawing, the tunnel in front of her led back toward the center of campus, winding under the gym, toward the administration building. The tunnel opposite went to the dorm next to the professor's house. Nancy pulled out the flashlight she had brought along and played it along the uneven ground. The light was just bright enough to show her the way.

Moving to the mouth of the tunnel, she bounced the small circle of light along the walls. Stepping carefully, her pumps slipped a little on the rocky foundation. From somewhere she heard a dripping noise. A broken pipe? she wondered. She touched the wall gingerly. It was dry.

There was an odd rustling in the corridor. Nancy swung the flashlight around her but saw nothing. The sound didn't repeat itself. Cautiously, she continued. There was a faint light ahead and she could tell that she was approaching another building.

The tunnel opened up and Nancy stepped

into another basement area, lit by a makeshift light, which was no more than a bare bulb attached to a long orange extension cord. The ground was sandier here. Bending down, she made out scuff marks in the dirt. So someone had been here before her! Nancy examined her map. She should be standing directly under the English building.

Could the scuff marks mean someone had come down from *this* building? The basement was empty, without even a fuse box to bring a maintenance worker there on legitimate business. Nancy tried the door. It was sealed shut.

The English building was the last exit before the long, dead-end corridor toward Adams Cottage. She tried to look down the tunnel, but the beam from the flashlight didn't penetrate very far into the darkness. The weak basement light illuminated only the first few feet of the tunnel, but she saw that the footprints led into it. Her muscles tensed.

As silently as possible, Nancy crept down the corridor. She doubted there was anyone down there with her, but she remembered the rustling she had heard. She wasn't going to take any chances. Gingerly, she stepped over the small rocks in the foundation floor.

It was getting harder to see, Nancy realized

suddenly. The light from the flashlight had dimmed considerably. She shook the flashlight but nothing happened. The batteries were fading. Looking behind her, she could no longer see the bulb from under the English building. She decided to forge ahead, anyway.

Shining the light ahead of her, she could see only two or three feet at the most. The tunnel unrolled before her in endless blackness.

The flashlight dimmed even more, and after she had gone only a few more feet, it flickered twice and died. With a sense of dread, Nancy fished out the penlight she always kept in her purse. Its thin beam barely pierced the blackness around her. She stood absolutely still, trying to picture the map in her mind. She couldn't be too far away from the dorm, she reasoned. It would be best to save the penlight for an emergency use and grope her way down the rest of the tunnel.

In the darkness the rustling sounded again behind her. Nancy's pulse pounded in her neck. Was there someone following her? The rustling stopped, but to her horror, Nancy heard a squeaking sound. It could only mean one thing: There had to be mice—or rats, even—in the tunnel with her.

She stopped and reached for the penlight, at the same time telling herself to stay calm. The rats weren't going to attack her, especially if she kept moving. She shone the thin beam ahead of her down the corridor.

Almost running now, she stumbled along the corridor. Her shoes made so much noise against the rough stones she couldn't tell if the rats were running with her. Stay calm, she told herself. You've been in worse situations. It wasn't a very comforting thought.

A rough stone caught the toe of one shoe. Before she could throw out a hand to stop herself, Nancy tripped and sprawled out, face forward, on the damp tunnel floor. The penlight flew from her hand and skidded over the stones. The faint light wavered and died as the tunnel was plunged into total darkness.

Nancy scrambled to her feet. With a sinking heart, she realized she had to keep moving. Unless . . . Trying to squelch her rising panic, she felt in her purse. She took out the map and folded it in half over and over until she had formed a little column of paper. Then she began to twist, until she had made a sort of paper candle. She dipped into her purse for the matchbook she had picked up when she and Ned and Angela were talking in the cafeteria. There were only two matches.

Cautiously, Nancy struck the first match. She heard a hiss and smelled sulfur, but nothing happened. She tried it again. Still the match wouldn't light. Blindly, she touched the match with her fingertip and felt the cardboard stem. She must have knocked the tip off when she struck it.

She had only one match now. She tore it out of the book and struck it on the flint strip. A tiny flame sprang up in front of her face. With great care, she touched it to the folded map and a glow grew into a light just big enough to see by. Holding up her hand to shield the makeshift candle from a draft, she scrambled through the corridor as quickly as she could.

The paper burned quickly. Soon there were only a few inches left. Then Nancy felt the ground even out under her feet. Something glinted dully off to her left. Breathlessly, she ran toward it. Just as she reached the source of light, the flame hit her fingers. She dropped the burning paper, and it fizzled on the cement. The darkness fell around her like a curtain, but it didn't matter now. She knew she was in the dorm basement.

Groping toward the dim reflection, Nancy found the door to the basement elevator. She tried the handle, but it didn't turn. This door hadn't been used lately; the elevator shaft was still sealed.

Nancy realized there might not be a way to get into the dorm from the tunnel. If not, she would have to retrace her steps back the way she had come, with no light this time, taking her chances with the rats. It wasn't something she looked forward to.

Nancy closed her eyes, trying to calm herself. Now she *was* panicking, she thought. From the ceiling to her left she spotted a very faint crack of light. Feeling her way in its direction, she banged her leg badly on something cold and hard. Cursing herself, she rubbed the sore leg, then explored whatever it was she'd bumped into.

Iron stairs! Leading up out of the tunnel. Relief flooded through her as she clambered up them. The glimmer of light she had noticed before formed the outline of a box now—a hatchway cover, Nancy realized. Holding her hands above her head, she fumbled for the latch. Her fingers scraped along the ceiling but finally she found it. She threw it to one side and pushed.

Light flooded the stairway. Squinting against the sudden shock of it, Nancy scrambled out and threw the trapdoor shut.

She was on a quiet lawn, outside the dorm. Resting for a moment, Nancy tried to quiet her pounding heart. Only a few yards from her was the tall, wrought iron fence that surrounded Emerson. Through the fence she could see the thick line of trees that separated the POE headquarters from the college.

As she rounded the corner of the dorm,

Nancy was more determined than ever to speak to Josef Maszak. The tunnel was the thief's most logical escape route, it had obviously been used recently, and it led almost to Maszak's door. One of those facts could be a coincidence —but all three? Nancy didn't think so.

Emerson's main entrance lay about one hundred yards away. And halfway between it and Nancy was Professor Maszak's house.

She marched up Maszak's steps and knocked briskly on the door. A face peered out through the curtains. Nancy lifted up her hand to knock again when the door swung open.

Maszak stared at Nancy. "Yes, Ms. Drew?"

"Professor Maszak," Nancy began boldly, "I have some questions, and I think you're the only one with the answers."

Maszak stepped back. "Please come in."

Nancy walked into a dim living room and sat in the chair he indicated. Maszak made no move to sit. Instead, he stood between her and the door.

"Well?"

Nancy took a deep breath. "Suppose we start with Jamison College," she said. "And the mysterious growth of that bacteria."

At Nancy's question, Maszak's face turned a deathly shade of white. Then he lunged for her, his hands outstretched. Maszak was going to strangle Nancy!

Chapter Twelve

NANCY PUT HER HANDS UP to protect herself. Maszak must have realized what he was about to do, because he pulled back, then threw himself into a chair facing her. He stared at Nancy in stunned surprise.

"The Jamison experiment—how did you find out?"

"I *am* a detective," Nancy said wryly.

As Nancy watched, Maszak's expression had changed from defiant anger to helpless defeat. He slumped deeper in his chair, and all his usual bluster faded. The professor looked drawn, even sickly.

"It was a brilliant discovery. And I couldn't pass up experiments with CLT. Yes, some of the CLT had come in contact with the bacteria and produced the abnormal growth. I've been terrified someone here would find out. Then you walked into my office, and I knew you were going to be trouble. I knew you'd uncover the theft."

"That's what I came here for," Nancy said.

Maszak shook his head impatiently. "No, not *this* theft. I mean the theft at Jamison."

The theft at Jamison? Nancy hid her confusion. "Well, the Jamison newspapers put two and two together for me," she bluffed.

"Ah, yes. Of course," the professor said sadly.

"Maybe you'd better start at the beginning," Nancy suggested, trying to sound as if she knew what Maszak was talking about.

Maszak nodded. "I came to America because of my wife's illness," he began. "It was very difficult to get all the necessary permission to teach here. Finally, because of my specialty, we were approved.

"We spent two and a half happy years at Jamison. Linda, my wife, was being treated successfully at the hospital. And I loved teaching."

"That wasn't the first time you began working with growth hormones, was it?" Nancy guessed.

"No, I worked with them in Hungary. It was

the first time I'd had such success, however. And then, just as things were ready to take off, someone stole the CLT."

"But no one ever knew what happened at Jamison," Nancy said, frowning. "Not even Dean Jarvis here at Emerson."

"No, he knew nothing." Maszak sighed. "It was terrible. I walked into my lab at Jamison one morning and the place was a shambles. Whoever broke in had torn the lab apart. The department head wanted to keep it quiet, though he requested a thorough list of everything that was stolen. Of course, I omitted the loss of the CLT."

"But if you didn't take it, why would you cover up the theft?" Nancy asked. "You might have stopped the thief then."

"I thought I would lose my job," the professor said miserably. "I was afraid because of my mistake with the bacteria that people would think I was extremely careless to have the CLT stolen, too. I couldn't afford to take the risk."

"No one would have blamed you for something beyond your control," Nancy assured him.

"Maybe, maybe not." Maszak shrugged. "I'm not used to your freedom here. I couldn't take the chance." He fell silent.

Nancy waited for him to continue. "Is that why you left Jamison?" she prompted.

"Yes. When Emerson applied for a visiting scientist, I asked to come here. But the thefts followed me."

Nancy was almost convinced that Maszak was telling the truth. Why would he risk his whole career and livelihood by stealing the CLT? Still, there was one thing that nagged at her. Nancy hesitated: "Professor, can you explain the argument I overheard you having yesterday on the pay phone?"

The professor reddened. "I was talking to the accountant at the hospital. Emerson hasn't sent the papers for us to be reimbursed by our health insurance yet. I owe a lot of money to the hospital still, but I don't think I should have to pay it with my money when my insurance covers it. The hospital will be paid eventually, but they want their money now. It's a mess."

Maszak could be accused of poor judgment, Nancy thought, but he didn't have to steal the CLT for money. He had insurance.

Nancy looked at Maszak, rumpled and slumped in his chair. She needed more information. Something still didn't make sense.

"Tell me, professor, how did you get involved with Bangs's group?" she asked innocently.

"Bangs's group? What group?" The professor looked genuinely blank.

"I mean POE," Nancy said slowly. "Philip Bangs was at Jamison at the same time the bacteria was discovered growing abnormally and the CLT was stolen. I don't think it's coincidence that he's here now, at the same time as the Emerson thefts."

Professor Maszak gave Nancy a startled look. "What do you mean?"

"I mean," Nancy replied patiently, "that Bangs is known for fighting technology that threatens the environment. He might feel the CLT threatens the future safety of animals. He might be after you to try to prevent you from continuing your experiments."

Maszak stared at her, and then a smile began to spread across his face. He was actually laughing!

"Ms. Drew," he said when he had gotten ahold of himself, "CLT doesn't harm the animals. It is only used to stimulate growth in cells. That's all."

Nancy was determined. "Professor, someone has tried very hard to get rid of me. There must be more to CLT than even you are aware of. Would you come with me to the lab? Maybe you'll see something I've missed."

Maszak gladly accompanied Nancy to the science building. Together, they combed the lab, though neither Maszak nor Nancy was sure what to look for.

"Look for anything that seems out of place," Nancy advised the professor as she stood in the walk-in freezer. "Or anything you've never seen before."

She scanned the third shelf from the bottom, where the CLT containers had been kept. She spotted a short, curly black hair frozen onto a shelf. Carefully, she chipped it off.

"I might take this to the police to be analyzed," she murmured. "Though it could belong to anyone—a student, a janitor, someone who had never even entered the lab."

"It is good to be thorough," the professor agreed.

"Do you have an envelope?" Nancy asked.

"An envelope? I must have an envelope somewhere." The professor looked around him helplessly. "I never realized I had so many papers."

"Here, let me look," Nancy offered. She began rummaging through his drawers.

They were crammed with test papers, lab books, copies of scientific articles. Nancy smiled to herself.

As she opened another drawer, Nancy noticed a piece of Maszak's stationery lying right on the top where it couldn't be missed. She picked it up by one corner. She was positive it hadn't been there before. In the center of the page, an address in Caracas, Venezuela, and three numbers had been neatly typed.

"Professor Maszak," Nancy asked, looking up, "what's this?"

Maszak looked at the paper in her hand. "I don't know," he answered. "I'm sure I've never seen it before."

Nancy looked at him questioningly. A man as messy as the professor couldn't really be trusted to remember which papers were his.

"No, I'm sure I've never seen it," Maszak said. He stared at the paper. "That is a date," he went on, "written European style, day first, month second." He frowned. "It's tomorrow's date. Why would someone put that in my drawer?"

Nancy looked at him thoughtfully. "It's my guess, professor, that the paper was planted by the thief."

"But why?" Maszak looked thoroughly puzzled.

"We don't know that yet," Nancy told him. "But if something were to happen tomorrow, maybe something dangerous or illegal, and this paper was found in your desk, it might be enough evidence to incriminate you."

Maszak shook his head impatiently. "I don't understand what you're saying."

Nancy grinned. "You can't frame someone with false information," she explained. "We have to assume this address has some real meaning. Now all we have to do is find out what that is—before tomorrow."

Maszak rubbed a hand over his forehead. "I'll be ruined. No one will ever hire me again."

Nancy placed a reassuring hand on Maszak's shoulder. "I don't know exactly how yet," she said, "but I'm convinced I can solve this whole puzzle."

She checked her watch. It was already midafternoon. "I've got to hurry, but don't worry," she told him. "I won't let anyone ruin your career."

Nancy left Maszak in his lab and hurried back to her dorm to pick up her car. Then she sped to Omega Chi to find Ned. Mike, Jan, and Amber Thomas were in the living room.

Jan and Amber sprang up as soon as they saw Nancy. "Thank goodness," Jan cried. "Ned called, and we didn't know how to reach you."

Mike struggled to stand up with his cane. "He said he was going to go over there," Mike said excitedly. "To POE headquarters. He thinks he's going to find Angela and bring her back."

"Is he there now?" Nancy asked.

"I'm not sure," Mike admitted. "He could be there, or he might still be at basketball practice. . . ." His voice trailed off. "Do you think I should go over there to see what's up?" he asked Nancy.

Nancy made a quick decision. "I have something to do first," she said, trying to soothe him. "If Ned already went to see Angela, he would have come right back. And besides, we don't know if he went there yet."

"I could find him," Mike suggested.

Walking with his cane, Nancy thought, Mike would be more of a problem than a help.

Her thoughts must have showed, for Mike suddenly looked embarrassed. "Just say the word, Nancy, and I'll do anything. If my best friend's in trouble, I'll help any way I can."

"You can help right now. I need directions to the police station in town," Nancy said.

Amber jumped up. "I know where it is. I have a friend who works there. Why don't Jan and I go with you?"

"Great," Nancy said enthusiastically. "And Mike, you wait here for Ned."

The three girls piled into the car and headed for town. Nancy was forcing herself not to worry about Ned. The information she needed now was crucial. Oh, Ned, she thought sadly, why couldn't you have waited until tomorrow to go to POE headquarters?

If Nancy's instincts were right, POE could be very dangerous. Even fatal.

Chapter Thirteen

AS THEY SPED TOWARD TOWN, Nancy tried to focus on the task ahead. The key to the mystery could be that address in Caracas. When she found out what it meant she would have the last answer to her questions. And the police had a computer that could give her that information.

The police station was a sprawling stone building in the center of Emersonville. Nancy parked and the three girls climbed the long low steps and hurried into the bustling receiving room.

Nancy racked her brain for some way to get access to the computer without giving away the case. At that moment, a handsome young sergeant with black hair strolled through the area.

"Joe!" Amber gave him a quick hug before turning to Nancy and Jan.

"This is Joe Ross," she said. "He'll help you, Nancy."

Joe flashed them a dazzling smile and ushered them down the hall. He was *very* handsome, Nancy decided. She glanced at Amber and saw the soft look in her lovely eyes. Clearly, Joe Ross was more than just a friend.

Joe held the computer room door open for them. "Jan says you need information about a foreign address," he said to Nancy. "But I don't see why you need the police."

Jan knew Nancy was a detective, but she didn't know Nancy was working on a case. With a quick glance at Amber and Joe, Nancy decided she had to break her cover to get the information she needed. Quickly she admitted she was really at Emerson to investigate a theft, leaving out details of Maszak's top secret experiment.

"I'm sorry I can't tell you more about the case," Nancy said sincerely, "but believe me, it's a matter of life or death. You can call the River Heights police to verify what I'm saying."

Joe looked abashed. "I'll have to," he admitted, "or I'll catch it."

He left the room to make the call. In a few

minutes he was back. "Okay," he said, turning to Nancy. "I'll help. What do you need?"

Nancy handed him a piece of paper. "I need to know who or what is at this address."

"Hmm." Joe frowned, running a hand absently through his glossy black hair. "The computer doesn't have a lot of information on foreign addresses, but let's see what it comes up with."

Joe sat down at one of the terminals and entered the address. "Here comes the information now."

Nancy read the computer screen. "The Shiranti Corporation. But who are they and what do they do? Can you find out for me?"

Joe looked apologetic. "I'll do my best," he declared. "But it'll take time. You'll have to wait."

"We don't have time," Nancy said, frowning. "Could you call me instead?"

After giving him phone numbers where she could be reached, Nancy thanked Joe, and the girls headed back to the car.

"Amber, you were a great help," Nancy said admiringly. "Thanks a lot."

"I enjoyed it," Amber said. "Being a detective is exciting."

"Especially when you get to see your boyfriend," Jan teased.

Nancy smiled distractedly as they got back in

the car and drove toward Emerson. Caracas, she mulled. Why was Caracas sending warning bells off in her mind? Then, in a flash, it hit her. South America. Angela said that Philip Bangs had settled in South America before coming back to the United States. She felt a tingle of excitement. All her hunches were playing out. Naturally Bangs, who headed antitechnology groups, would want to destroy the CLT if it harmed animals. He might even destroy it as part of the demonstration Angela had said POE was planning against Senator Claiborne.

"Amber." Nancy glanced at her excitedly. "The minute we get back to Emerson, would you call Joe and see what he learned about the Shiranti Corporation?"

At Amber's confused look, Nancy explained her suspicions about POE. Both girls continued to look dumbfounded but promised to help any way they could.

As soon as they got back to Emerson, Amber disappeared to call Joe. "Here goes," she said when she returned. "Joe found out the Shiranti Corporation is owned by a Caracas family by the name of Rojas. Shiranti is a pharmaceutical company. Does that help?"

Nancy frowned. "Pharmaceuticals," she repeated. "Drugs and medicines."

"Right," Amber said. "They supply drugs to Third World countries to fight disease."

A thrill shot down Nancy's spine. Leaping to her feet, she grabbed Amber in a hug.

"That's it!" she exclaimed. "Amber, you just cracked the case. I've got to call Dean Jarvis right away."

Since it was late Nancy had to call the dean at home. She arranged to meet him in his office in five minutes. Leaving Jan and Amber to wait in the dorm for any word from Ned, she hurried to the administration building. She was waiting on the front stairs in the early twilight when Dean Jarvis arrived. Nancy followed him past the night watchman in the lobby and waited while he unlocked his office and closed the door behind them.

"Dean Jarvis," she began, "you told me you get copies of Maszak's experiment logs every day. I need to see where you keep them."

The dean looked distressed. "Why, I keep everything in a locked file." He showed Nancy the filing cabinet.

"No one can get into it," he insisted. "Plus, my office door is locked. And the guard outside is on duty every night at six P.M."

"What about during school hours when you *are* here?" Nancy pressed patiently.

"Well, uh," the dean hedged. "No one is going to slip into my office unnoticed, if that's what you mean."

"Yes, that is what I mean," Nancy said. "Our

culprit needs constant access to those files to know when the professor has finished treating the CLT. What about your secretary?"

"She's been with me for fifteen years," the dean said hotly. "If she was going to steal secrets, she could certainly have started long before this."

Nancy kept her voice cool and neutral, trying not to alarm the dean more than he already was. "But it could have been someone else who works here, someone dropping things off, delivering messages or packages. You told me yourself, this place is full of people during the day. You couldn't possibly keep your eye on all of them."

The dean dropped his head into his hands and groaned. "You're right," he said. "And I keep everything in that file—everything our thief would need. The schedule of CLT shipments, the codes for the combination locks, notes on the experiment, everything!"

"If someone who works here is working with the thief, it would certainly explain how they knew when I was in the lab closet," Nancy continued. "I told you on the telephone exactly where all of us would be that night. He could have listened in."

The dean looked devastated. "I put your life in danger," he said softly. "I'm terribly sorry." He rummaged through his desk and drew out a list of names. "Here. This is everyone who works here."

Nancy scanned the list. She stopped at the *L*'s. She had found what she was looking for.

Karen Lewis.

"Karen Lewis works in this office?"

The dean nodded. "Yes, for the past five semesters." He shook his head in confusion. "She's a terrific worker, a great kid. I can't believe she'd be mixed up in something illegal."

Nancy nodded. "I know," she said, remembering how concerned Karen had been over the injured dog at the infirmary. "It is hard to believe."

Promising the dean she would explain more later, Nancy ran back to Ned's fraternity house. She burst in to find Mike O'Shea pacing the floor.

"Nancy!" he cried out as she walked in the door. "I heard from Ned, but it doesn't sound good."

Nancy's heart contracted in fear. "What do you mean?"

Mike rubbed his face in agitation. "One of our frat brothers took a phone message from Ned. It was for you, but he left a number, so I called it."

"What did Ned say?"

Distressed, Mike shook his head. "That's just it—Ned didn't say anything. Someone picked up, but then there was silence on the other end. When I said hello, the phone went dead."

"Mike, give me the number," Nancy cried. With trembling fingers, Nancy dialed. The phone rang once, and someone lifted the receiver. There was silence.

Nancy took a deep breath to steady her voice. "This is Nancy Drew speaking," she said.

A distorted voice came over the wire.

"How lovely to hear from you," the voice said. "We have your boyfriend here, Ms. Drew. But if you don't drop your investigation and leave Emerson immediately, you'll never see him again."

Chapter Fourteen

HER HAND TREMBLING, Nancy put down the receiver. The eerie voice echoed in her ears.

"Was that Ned?" Mike cried. "What's going on?"

Nancy wet her lips, trying to get the words out. "They have Ned," she said in a choked voice. "They threatened me. They said if I don't drop the case now, I'll never see him again."

Mike exploded. "I knew something was wrong," he said. "I should have gone looking for him."

During the conversation Jan and Amber had come in. Jan hurried to Mike's side. "I'm glad you stayed here," she said to console him. "Whoever it is sounds dangerous. Besides, we can help Ned more if we're all together. Right, Nancy?"

They all turned to look at Nancy. She was only dimly aware of them. The disembodied voice was stuck in her head, the warning running over and over again.

"I'm going to call the police," Amber blurted out.

Nancy suddenly sprang back to life. "No," she cried. "Don't. I believe that voice. If we call the police, we may never get Ned out of there."

"Then what are we going to do?" Amber looked as if she might cry, and for a second, Nancy was afraid she might burst into tears herself. With tremendous effort, she forced herself to act stronger than she felt.

"*We* aren't going to do anything," she said finally. "*I'm* going over there alone to try to get him out."

"You're not leaving me behind," Mike declared. "Not when my best friend's life is in danger!"

"And we won't let you go alone," Jan added. "It's too dangerous."

"Thanks, Jan," Nancy answered, "but the more people there are, the more likely it is that they'll spot us." Nancy didn't want to remind Mike that with his bad leg, he would be less of a help than a hindrance. "I've got to go alone."

"Oh, no, you won't," Jan declared hotly. "You need some kind of backup, and Amber and I are coming. We won't stay behind, so you might as well agree now."

One look at Jan's face told Nancy it was useless to argue.

"Okay," she said. "The two of you come with me. Mike, you can do more good by staying here to sound the alarm if we aren't back soon. Okay?"

Mike looked at her without replying but made no move to follow them out the door.

The girls got into Nancy's car. Without speaking, they drove to POE's headquarters. There were a number of cars parked along the driveway near the entrance. Nancy pulled up behind them.

"I'll have to park on the curb," she said. "We don't want anyone blocking us in."

Getting out of the car, Nancy took a deep breath. She was more shaken than she wanted to admit. The strain of worrying about Ned was making it hard for her to concentrate. And right then she needed to concentrate, more than ever.

The sun had finished setting and the moon was almost full. Its light bathed the trees around them and exposed the buildings clearly.

"What do we do?" Amber asked quietly.

As clearly as she could, Nancy explained the layout of the place, trying to remember as much as possible from her brief visit there.

"If they're holding Ned here, he's probably in one of the smaller buildings they use for sleeping," Nancy explained in a whisper. "I'm going into the large warehouse building," she continued. "If I haven't come out in ten minutes, get out of here—fast. If you find Ned, take him with you and go for help."

"Nancy, it's not safe to leave you alone," Jan protested.

"You'll have to," Nancy said quietly. "I'm not just here to rescue Ned." She had to pause to wet her lips again. "I've got to stop a thief, too."

For a long moment Amber and Jan looked at each other in silence.

"Be careful," Jan finally whispered.

"You, too," Nancy replied.

Nancy had never felt so alone as she did watching Jan and Amber go. Part of her wanted desperately to go with them, to find Ned and forget about CLT and Philip Bangs and the rest of them. But there might be a lot more at stake than just Ned's safety.

She forced herself to wait until Jan and Amber disappeared safely into the first low-lying building. She was about to rise from her crouched position when headlights lit up the drive. A car swung into the driveway, and Nancy ducked behind the tree line.

The car backed off a bit and pulled to the side of the drive. It must be a member, she thought, waiting for someone to emerge from the car, but no one got out. She was going to have to pass right in front of it to get to the doorway.

Lying flat, Nancy began inching her way along the ground. Keeping to the shadows, she made her way toward the main building. It was ablaze with light. The sound of many voices talking drifted outside.

There definitely was a meeting going on, which explained why all the cars were there. Nancy crept around the side of the building and surveyed the path to the front door. Three or four students were hanging out in the entrance. She had to get past them, as well as stand up in front of whoever was waiting in the car on the drive. She'd have to risk it.

Nancy remembered the earring Sara had found in the lab. She still had it in her purse. She slipped it on. Maybe she could pass as a member.

The students around the door barely glanced at her as she walked past them into the room. Breathing a sigh of relief, she crept toward the back of the room and took a seat on a straw mat.

The audience now sat patiently facing an empty podium, waiting expectantly and occasionally murmuring softly to one another. As Nancy watched, a young man got up and stood before the crowd. Nancy recognized him as Bob, the guy she thought was hurt on the road her first day at Emerson.

"Greetings, brothers and sisters," he called. "Now that the preliminaries are out of the way, let's get down to business. It's time to talk about tomorrow's demonstration."

Around Nancy, the crowd burst into loud cheers.

"Tomorrow is a historic occasion for all of us," Bob continued. He paced back and forth in front of them. "Tomorrow, we will capture the attention of the nation. When we stage our protest against Senator Claiborne, the country will know that POE means business. Someone has to protect our environment, and we're the ones to start doing it!"

The students around Nancy jumped to their feet, yelling and waving their arms. Awkwardly, Nancy followed their lead.

She realized they were discussing the plan for their faked gun battle.

"Listen carefully," Bob called when the crowd had quieted. "This event must be carefully orchestrated. You all must do exactly what you're told. Remember, you have a job to do. Now, we need a head count. Everyone who has volunteered as a 'victim,' raise your hand."

As hands went up, Nancy realized she had sat in the middle of a group of victims. To her horror, Karen Lewis got up in front of the meeting to count the hands. Nancy hunched her shoulders and looked down, hoping to escape notice.

"Thank you," Bob called as the count was taken. "The water guns for the attackers are in the closet at the back of the room. All of you who are attackers, pick up a gun and make sure you bring it to the auditorium tomorrow by four-thirty P.M. Don't attract attention by talking together or loitering in the halls."

"Victims" and "attackers," Nancy thought. Exactly what were they planning to do? And what did the demonstration have to do with the CLT?

"Finally," Bob called, "and this is the most important thing—it must look absolutely real. We will warn the senator that unless he puts an end to his reckless plans to destroy our parkland, there will be war in this country. We want him to think this is really happening. I want the people around you screaming in terror. I want them to believe that unless they stop Senator Claiborne and others like him, they'll see a war in this nation and blood on their hands!"

Nancy stared in astonishment. Didn't they realize how dangerous their plan was? If the campus police thought they were using real guns for a real attack, they could begin firing. Most likely, the rest of the audience would panic. It would be absolute chaos. People might be seriously hurt, even killed. Didn't anyone see the danger in that?

Stunned, Nancy looked at the students caught up in their fervor. Obviously, not one of them was thinking clearly.

In the middle of her despair, Nancy noticed Karen Lewis get up and go down the stairs to the basement. Had she recognized Nancy? Getting up quietly, Nancy slipped away from the group and followed Karen.

At the bottom of the stairs, Nancy had to choose between a long hallway that stretched straight ahead and one that veered off to the left. Each hallway had a series of doors along it. At the end of the straight corridor, Nancy saw a thin line of light under a door.

Nancy crept toward the light, flattening herself along the wall and peering into the windows in each door. Through one window, Nancy recognized lab equipment on a counter. Her heart began to pound.

But the room was empty. Nancy continued searching for Karen. Anxiously, she quickened her pace. There was only one door left, at the very end of the hall. She heard nothing from inside.

Taking a deep breath, she slowly pushed the door with her foot. It swung open immediately. The sound of her pounding heart seemed to fill the corridor. When no one reacted to the open door, Nancy gathered her courage and burst inside. Her eyes widened.

On the floor in the corner, their hands tied and their mouths gagged, were Angela and Ned. And they weren't moving!

Chapter Fifteen

NANCY CRASHED THROUGH THE DOOR.

Quickly she rushed to untie them. Not only were they gagged and their hands tied behind their backs but their feet were lashed together as well. Someone was making sure they couldn't even *try* to escape.

Nancy pulled Ned's gag off first.

"Ned," she whispered desperately. "Ned, can you talk? It's me, Nancy."

Ned groaned faintly but made no attempt to speak. They were drugged, Nancy realized. She turned to work on Angela's gag. Gently, she slapped Angela's face. No response. Without their help, she'd never get them out. They were much too heavy to carry.

Amber and Jan would be peeking in the meeting room any minute, but they'd never know to look for Nancy in the basement. And if she went upstairs to get them, something could happen to Ned and Angela while she was gone. Karen Lewis might already be rounding up people to stop her.

As Nancy untied Ned's hands and propped him up against the wall her mind was racing. She'd intended to search for the CLT, but now that she'd found Ned and Angela she could hardly abandon them—and she certainly didn't want to.

Ned's handsome face was slack and a dark bruise swelled on his right cheekbone.

"Ned, oh, Ned, please wake up," she pleaded softly. His eyelids fluttered briefly. "That's it, Ned," she encouraged him. "You've got to help me."

She had bent to loosen the ropes around his feet when she heard the sound of footsteps in the corridor outside. Nancy whirled, searching out a hiding place. Just in time, she ducked behind a stack of cartons.

Karen Lewis stood in the doorway.

"What is this? Ned, Angela?" Karen cried in disbelief. "Oh, no—what happened to you?" From the tone in her voice, Karen seemed genuinely distressed. Nancy peered behind the boxes to see Karen rush to Ned's side, her hand over her mouth.

"Ned," Karen whispered, bending over him. "Can you hear me? Who did this to you?"

Relief flooded through Nancy. Karen had no part in tying up Angela or Ned. She stood up.

"Karen," she whispered desperately. "Don't be alarmed—you've got to help me get them out of here. It's Bangs, he—" The words died in her throat.

Philip Bangs was standing in the doorway. Coolly, he surveyed the room, a wide smile spreading across his face.

"Good evening, Ms. Drew," he drawled. "You caught us at an awkward moment."

Nancy took a step out from behind the cartons. "Don't move," Bangs ordered. Turning to Karen, he said, "Don't panic, Karen. Everything will be all right if you do just as I say. Go wrap up that meeting. Get everyone out of here—before our girl detective tries anything else."

Wordlessly, Karen left the room. At the doorway, she turned, throwing Nancy a look she couldn't decipher.

"You should have left when you had the chance," Bangs said casually. He gestured to the unmoving figures of Ned and Angela. "Now you've put their lives in jeopardy."

"They have nothing to do with this," Nancy exclaimed. "I'm the only one who knows about the CLT."

To her satisfaction, Bangs started at the mention of the chemical. "You have figured it out, then." He grinned and saluted her. "You're more clever than I suspected."

"Let them go, Bangs," Nancy bargained. "I'll help you get away if you do."

Bangs cocked an eyebrow at her. "Will you, now? I'm afraid that's impossible. Your friend Ned here asked a few too many questions about me. So you're lying, Ms. Drew—you're not the only one who knows about CLT." Reaching behind him, Bangs drew a gun from the waistband of his pants.

Inwardly, Nancy groaned. Poor Ned. In trying to help her and Angela, he had put himself —and Nancy—in even greater danger.

"First, come out from behind those cartons where I can see you," Bangs directed. "Sit cross-legged on the floor over there."

Nancy stepped out from the desk and sat beside Ned.

"Not there. Over there," Bangs screamed, taking a step toward her. Quickly, Nancy scooted away.

"That's better. You think he's going to wake up and help you, but you're wrong," Bangs muttered. He walked over to Ned and nudged him roughly with his foot. Ned didn't make a sound.

Nancy cringed. "You're going to pay for this, Bangs," she promised.

Bangs smiled. "Will I? I doubt it. You may be smart, but don't forget I'm smarter. I masterminded this whole thing single-handedly. In fact, POE was created specifically to steal the CLT. Quite clever, I think, when you realize none of the members have any idea what the stuff really is. After all, who would believe that an antitechnology group was stealing an extraordinarily dangerous biological weapon?"

"No one," Nancy said, playing along with the game. She had suspected the true nature of CLT, but Bangs had just confirmed it for her.

Bangs chuckled. "So, you knew what the CLT really was, then. Perhaps you're smarter than I thought."

Nancy pretended to be as cool as Bangs. "Of course," she said. "Once I put the Shiranti Corporation together with the time you were at Jamison, I knew what you were up to. CLT affects bacteria in the same way it affects animals.

"You heard about Maszak's 'accident'—that his growth hormone got mixed up in a rheumatic fever culture and that the disease began growing out of control—and that's why you're so interested in it," Nancy said grimly. "Because a disease that spread so fast could wipe out whole towns at once."

Bangs looked delighted at the thought. "And the best part is, it would be impossible to trace. If you planted CLT in a city water system the relatively harmless bacteria already there would create an immediate plague. No one would know where it came from. Particularly if the hormone itself was shipped in by a well-known pharmaceutical company—along with its regular supply of medicine." Bangs rubbed his hands together gleefully.

Nancy was sickened by Bangs's twisted mind.

"The world is full of dangerous bacteria, Ms. Drew," he said happily. "And CLT would have the same effect on any number of them. We have to thank Maszak for that—his treatment is the key. Somehow, he makes the hormone compatible with the bacteria."

"Yes, something only Maszak knows," Nancy said thoughtfully. "The lab here—you've been using your medical background to try to duplicate Maszak's treatment. But you haven't found it," Nancy stated, realizing the whole truth at once. "If you had, you would have left Emerson a long time ago."

"A nosy girl detective and her macho boyfriend put a little kink in my plans," Bangs said savagely. "But not for long. Karen works in the dean's office. She'll continue to feed me

Maszak's files. Bob is a clever engineering student—he made the tunnels usable for me. I have many people helping, you see. And all in the name of a good cause—saving the world from Maszak's biological weapon."

"You're very clever," Nancy conceded.

Bangs nodded proudly. "You did give me a scare," he said generously. He glanced at Ned and Angela. "I was hoping she would help steal the secret. As a biochem major, she knew the lab, and no one would have suspected her questions. But unfortunately, your friend Ned made her a little suspicious. When Angela learned I was taking the CLT, she tried to warn Maszak. Luckily, I got her away in time."

"But not before she left a clue behind," Nancy said, pulling on the earring she was wearing.

Bangs shrugged. "I almost had her convinced we were taking CLT as a blow against biotechnology everywhere. None of these silly students knows the real reason."

"There are an awful lot of students involved," Nancy said. "You can't keep them in the dark forever."

"I don't need to," Bangs replied. "The little disturbance tomorrow will probably mark the end of POE, anyway. The school will ban them after a stunt like the gun battle they have planned."

"People could be killed," Nancy said coldly.

Bangs shrugged. "If they are, no one will be thinking about my little theft, will they?"

Nancy was revolted. Bangs was a madman, but she had to keep him talking until Ned woke up, or until Amber and Jan brought help.

"So now what?" she asked. "You still don't know the formula. What are you going to do about that?"

"Forget the formula," he said angrily. "I don't need it. I can sell the CLT and cut my losses. I'll still be a billionaire." Bangs waved his gun toward Ned and Angela. "And only the three of you stand in my way."

Nancy licked her lips. "I admire your plan, Bangs," she said, bluffing. "Maybe we could work together."

Bangs frowned. "I always work alone. And I'm wasting time. Say goodbye, Nancy Drew." He aimed the gun at Nancy's head.

Suddenly a figure flew out of the doorway at Bangs, knocking him backward—Karen Lewis. She must have stayed outside the door and listened to the whole conversation.

As Nancy leapt toward Bangs, Karen struggled with him. The gun went off, and Karen sank to the ground, clutching at her left arm. Bangs dropped the gun and fled down the hall.

Nancy knelt by Karen's side. "Karen, are you okay?"

The other girl nodded. "Get Bangs," she gasped. "Don't let him get away."

Nancy hesitated.

"I'm okay," Karen insisted. "Go!"

Karen was right, Nancy knew. If she didn't go now, she was going to lose Bangs. With a last look behind her, Nancy sprinted down the hall. She raced up the stairs, two at a time, and sprang into the meeting room.

The place was in an uproar. The students milled about in confusion, bewildered by the sight of Bangs running out of the building. Nancy desperately pushed her way past them. She burst through in time to see Bangs jump into his car. "Let me through," Nancy cried.

The crowd swelled around her. She couldn't get out!

Chapter Sixteen

"NANCY, WHAT HAPPENED?"

Amber and Jan pushed through the crowd toward Nancy.

"Did you find Ned?" Jan asked, panting.

"Or the CLT?" Amber whispered.

"No time to explain," Nancy gasped. "Get me out of here!"

Together, the three girls pushed a clearing through the crowd and made it outside.

Nancy's mind raced. Bangs had left without the CLT. That meant he didn't have it in the building. He must be on his way to get it now.

"Amber, Jan—listen. Ned and Angela are inside. Karen Lewis is there, too. She's been shot. You'll need to get her to a doctor right away."

Amber gasped, but Nancy went on. "Karen is on our side. They're all downstairs, last door on your right. I'm going after Bangs. I don't think anyone else will bother you—but hurry!"

Leaving Amber and Jan gaping after her, Nancy sprinted toward her car.

"Be careful," Amber shouted after her. "Bangs could be dangerous."

She had no idea *how* dangerous, Nancy thought.

Gunning the motor, Nancy drove as fast as she dared, headed for the one place where Bangs could have hidden the CLT.

A glare in her rearview mirror caught her attention. A car's headlights were directly behind her.

Could one of Bangs's henchmen be following her?

It was impossible to see who was behind the wheel. Nancy told herself it was probably just a student leaving the meeting. Bangs hadn't had enough time to instruct anyone to follow her.

Turning onto campus, Nancy swept past the security check post. The guard leapt out when she failed to stop, but she kept on going. The car following her reached the security booth. With a quick glance in the rearview mirror, Nancy saw the other car come to a complete halt. The driver leaned out his window, and he and the guard exchanged words.

It was no one, Nancy thought with relief. Just a student leaving the meeting.

Determined now, she sped toward the cafeteria, the one place on campus where Bangs could have hidden the CLT. After the exploding doorknob incident, the campus police had searched the cafeteria thoroughly. Nothing had been stolen, she remembered, but no one had checked to see if anything had been *left* there.

Pulling into the parking lot at the rear of the building, near the cafeteria kitchen, Nancy braked next to Bangs's red sports car. The cafeteria windows were dark, but the door to the kitchen stood ajar. Holding her breath, Nancy slipped inside. The open door of the walk-in freezer threw a halo of light onto Philip Bangs.

Nancy spotted the light switch and flipped it on. "You won't get away this time," she cried.

Bangs froze, caught in the act of hauling a shiny cylinder of CLT out of the freezer. For a moment he did nothing. Then he bent down abruptly and rolled one of the three huge canisters directly at her.

Just as it was almost on top of her, Nancy

jumped, clearing the canister completely. Bangs actually laughed out loud.

"Very clever," he drawled, advancing upon her.

Nancy drew back and surprised Bangs with a karate kick that sent him spinning. He plowed into a rack of pots and pans, which banged and clattered onto the floor. He recovered quickly and ran toward her again.

Nancy assumed her fighting stance, preparing to fend off a blow. Instead, as he was almost close enough to reach her, Bangs launched himself toward the counter on Nancy's right, reaching for a heavy carving board.

Bangs grabbed the board and slashed it through the air, aiming at Nancy's head. She jumped back but he kept on coming, his arm swinging the block wildly, challenging her.

Bangs advanced and Nancy retreated. He was backing her into a corner, she realized, where she would be trapped. She flung out an arm to ward off his attack and her hand knocked into a box mounted on the wall. A fire alarm, Nancy realized!

If she pulled it, help would come—if she could elude Bangs until then. At the same moment as she moved to pull the lever, Bangs realized what she was doing. He threw himself at the alarm box.

In the same second Nancy spied a frying pan lying a few feet away. She leapt at it even as Bangs was bringing the carving board down onto the glass face of the fire alarm. The glass shattered and the board splintered from the force of the blow.

Sickened as she realized how narrowly she'd escaped that blow herself, Nancy swung the heavy iron pan into the backs of Bangs's legs. His knees buckled and his feet slid out from under him. Bangs fell, crying out in pain and surprise. Her heart pounding, Nancy backed off, waving the pan threateningly above her head.

The kitchen door burst open and two police officers rushed into the room.

"Freeze," one of them shouted, pointing his gun uncertainly, first at Nancy, then at Bangs.

"Not her—him! The one on the floor," a voice from the door directed.

Nancy whirled in surprise. "Mike O'Shea," she gasped breathlessly. "What are you doing here?"

"Well, I couldn't sit around and do nothing," Mike said cheerfully to the crowd.

With Ned's arm securely around her shoulder, Nancy grinned happily from the loveseat. They were in the living room of Ned's frat house, with Amber and Jan sprawled on the sofa, and Karen and Angela perched on pillows by the fireplace.

Sitting in the peaceful room, it was hard to believe that only hours before, they had all been involved in a life-or-death struggle.

"Tell us, Mike," Ned ordered. "How *did* you end up at the kitchen just when Nancy needed you?"

"With two police officers in tow," Nancy added.

Mike grinned bashfully. "It was easy. After Nancy and the girls left, I followed them," Mike explained. "I figured someone better keep an eye on them. I drove after them to POE headquarters and parked along the edge of the road to wait."

"So that was *you* in the car I saw!" Nancy exclaimed in surprise.

"Right," Mike confirmed with a smile. "When Bangs's car peeled out of there, I didn't know what to do. But when I saw you tearing down the driveway, I decided to give you some backup, just in case. I know you're a famous detective and all"—Mike grinned—"but I figured, once in a while, everyone needs a little help from their friends."

"You figured right," Nancy said wryly. She felt Ned's arm tighten around her.

"Anyway," Mike went on, "I stopped at the security gate and told them to call the police."

"And a good thing, too," Ned declared. "But Nancy, how did you guess where Bangs was headed?"

"It was easy, once I realized he didn't have the CLT."

With the mystery solved, Nancy had felt free to fill in the others on all the details.

"I reasoned he didn't have it, because he hadn't been able to get it off campus," she continued. "There aren't too many places you can hide something that big, and frozen, too. Then I remembered the doorknobs."

Angela looked blank. "I don't think I've heard this part."

Nancy smiled at her. "Bangs put an explosive on the doorknob to my closet. He thought he'd scare me away."

"Never!" Ned declared comically.

Grinning, Nancy continued. "I talked to the security men, and they said three other doors on campus had been blown up, too. One of them was the door to the cafeteria. The other two doors, which were to the library and the computer room, were probably hit to disguise the real target."

Jan frowned, looking puzzled. "Then he must have blasted his way in there after he had stolen the CLT."

"Exactly," Nancy agreed. "The tunnels were

the real clue—they connect all the *original* buildings on campus. The cafeteria is a modern building, so there was no way to get in from below. Bangs had to blast his way in there to store the stolen CLT."

Mike whistled. "Pretty clever guy."

"Very clever," Nancy agreed. "My guess is he stored the CLT in the cafeteria for a few days until he could get it safely across the street."

For a moment nobody spoke. Then Karen Lewis let out an anguished moan.

"How could I have been so stupid?" she cried. "I should have known what was going on." She stared down at her hands. Tears began to well up in her eyes.

The others exchanged uncomfortable glances, except for Angela.

"It wasn't your fault," Angela told Karen sympathetically. "He fooled me, too. I thought Bangs wanted to save the world, not destroy it."

Karen nodded and wiped the tears from her eyes. "It's sad, really. In the beginning, we were so full of purpose. I thought POE would do great things. Somehow, helping Philip steal the CLT seemed like the right thing to do. The way he explained it, being chosen for his 'special mission' was a real honor." She spat out the words bitterly. "I never realized what I was getting into."

"That's why I was so worried about Angela," Ned said quietly. "Sometimes, you can get carried away in a group and not even know right from wrong anymore."

"I was in too deep, I guess," Karen said. "Suddenly things were going too fast for me to think clearly. And," she added, looking ashamed, "I guess I wanted to please Philip."

"He's a pretty forceful guy," Nancy put in. "He could have used that power for good, but unfortunately he chose to use it for evil instead."

Karen looked up with fresh tears in her eyes. "But I'm still to blame for a lot of it," she declared. "I helped form the group; I went along with everything he said."

"You didn't know what he was really doing," Ned pointed out.

"No," Karen admitted, "but that doesn't make me feel any better." She gave a weak smile. "I still feel like I got off too easily."

"You got hurt," Amber exclaimed. "That's not 'easily,' if you ask me."

"And you did save us," Angela added, "I mean, in the end."

Karen looked up with a newly determined look on her face. "There is something I can do," she announced. "I can stop the demonstration tomorrow. There won't be any guns in the auditorium, fake or not. And I can turn POE back into the group it should be—a peaceful group, one committed to truly protecting our environment."

Angela turned to Ned, her eyes sparkling. "That's a wonderful idea," she said. "And I'll bet the first one to join your *new* group will be Ned Nickerson."

Nancy gave Ned a special squeeze as everyone laughed.

As Professor Maszak invited Nancy and Ned into his freshly cleaned living room, he was positively jovial.

"Sit down, sit down," he urged. "Can I get you anything?"

"Thanks, but we can stay only a minute," Nancy replied. "I just came to say goodbye."

"I'm so glad you did! I can thank you again for all you've done," the professor said. "I even have a bit of good news. My assistant, Sara—she got her scholarship." Maszak's eyes twinkled. "Now maybe she'll be able to relax and stop blowing things up in the lab."

"I'm sure she will," Nancy said warmly.

"But seriously," he continued, "I want you to know something else. I have realized that nothing can ever justify unleashing my formula on the world again—accidentally *or* on purpose. I destroyed it this morning. I wiped it out of the computer and burned all my notes. And I promise you, I will never create it again."

"But, professor," Nancy asked, "does that ruin your chances of teaching at Emerson?"

"No, no, that's the best part," Maszak said. "Emerson has offered me tenure! My job is now permanent. So what do you think, Ned?" the professor teased. "Maybe next semester, you'll take one of my classes?"

Ned laughed. "No thanks, sir. Your classes are too dangerous for me!"

After saying their goodbyes, Nancy and Ned strolled back to her dorm.

"Well, Nan, I guess you finally have a little free time on your hands." Tenderly, Ned brushed a strand of hair from her eyes.

Nancy smiled. "Did you have anything particular in mind?"

Ned's brown eyes lingered on her face. "I think I owe you one dinner. Why don't you go slip into that silk dress of yours—"

"No way!" Nancy cried. "Every time we split up, something happens. Let's play it safe. We'll order a pizza and eat it in my room—together."

"You mean—alone together, don't you?" Ned teased, taking her hand.

"Alone together," Nancy promised as she tilted her face to meet his kiss.

Nancy's next case:

A beautiful young woman in nearby Mapleton has been bilking the members of a posh country club out of thousands of dollars. The extortionist's name, according to the victims, is Nancy Drew! What's worse, the con artist is a dead ringer for the teen detective.

The fix is in, and Nancy feels the sting. But two can play at this con game. Disguising herself as a reporter, Nancy resolves to ferret out the truth. The story's hot, but the news is all bad. A small-time Chicago hood has turned up dead with Nancy Drew's name in his pocket, and now the police suspect her of murder . . . in *FALSE IMPRESSIONS*, Case #43 in The Nancy Drew Files™.